LEFT

TO

PREY

(An Adele Sharp Mystery—Book Eleven)

BLAKE PIERCE

Blake Pierce

Blake Pierce is the USA Today bestselling author of the RILEY PAGE mystery series, which includes seventeen books. Blake Pierce is also the author of the MACKENZIE WHITE mystery series, comprising fourteen books; of the AVERY BLACK mystery series, comprising six books; of the KERI LOCKE mystery series, comprising five books; of the MAKING OF RILEY PAIGE mystery series, comprising six books; of the KATE WISE mystery series, comprising seven books; of the CHLOE FINE psychological suspense mystery, comprising six books; of the JESSE HUNT psychological suspense thriller series, comprising nineteen books; of the AU PAIR psychological suspense thriller series, comprising three books; of the ZOE PRIME mystery series, comprising six books; of the ADELE SHARP mystery series, comprising thirteen books, of the EUROPEAN VOYAGE cozy mystery series, comprising four books; of the new LAURA FROST FBI suspense thriller, comprising six books (and counting); of the new ELLA DARK FBI suspense thriller, comprising nine books (and counting); of the A YEAR IN EUROPE cozy mystery series, comprising nine books, of the AVA GOLD mystery series, comprising six books (and counting); and of the RACHEL GIFT mystery series, comprising six books (and counting).

An avid reader and lifelong fan of the mystery and thriller genres, Blake loves to hear from you, so please feel free to visit www.blakepierceauthor.com to learn more and stay in touch.

BOOKS BY BLAKE PIERCE

RACHEL GIFT MYSTERY SERIES
HER LAST WISH (Book #1)
HER LAST CHANCE (Book #2)
HER LAST HOPE (Book #3)
HER LAST FEAR (Book #4)
HER LAST CHOICE (Book #5)
HER LAST BREATH (Book #6)

AVA GOLD MYSTERY SERIES
CITY OF PREY (Book #1)
CITY OF FEAR (Book #2)
CITY OF BONES (Book #3)
CITY OF GHOSTS (Book #4)
CITY OF DEATH (Book #5)
CITY OF VICE (Book #6)

A YEAR IN EUROPE
A MURDER IN PARIS (Book #1)
DEATH IN FLORENCE (Book #2)
VENGEANCE IN VIENNA (Book #3)
A FATALITY IN SPAIN (Book #4)

ELLA DARK FBI SUSPENSE THRILLER
GIRL, ALONE (Book #1)
GIRL, TAKEN (Book #2)
GIRL, HUNTED (Book #3)
GIRL, SILENCED (Book #4)
GIRL, VANISHED (Book 5)
GIRL ERASED (Book #6)
GIRL, FORSAKEN (Book #7)
GIRL, TRAPPED (Book #8)
GIRL, EXPENDABLE (Book #9)

LAURA FROST FBI SUSPENSE THRILLER

ALREADY GONE (Book #1)
ALREADY SEEN (Book #2)
ALREADY TRAPPED (Book #3)
ALREADY MISSING (Book #4)
ALREADY DEAD (Book #5)
ALREADY TAKEN (Book #6)

EUROPEAN VOYAGE COZY MYSTERY SERIES
MURDER (AND BAKLAVA) (Book #1)
DEATH (AND APPLE STRUDEL) (Book #2)
CRIME (AND LAGER) (Book #3)
MISFORTUNE (AND GOUDA) (Book #4)
CALAMITY (AND A DANISH) (Book #5)
MAYHEM (AND HERRING) (Book #6)

ADELE SHARP MYSTERY SERIES
LEFT TO DIE (Book #1)
LEFT TO RUN (Book #2)
LEFT TO HIDE (Book #3)
LEFT TO KILL (Book #4)
LEFT TO MURDER (Book #5)
LEFT TO ENVY (Book #6)
LEFT TO LAPSE (Book #7)
LEFT TO VANISH (Book #8)
LEFT TO HUNT (Book #9)
LEFT TO FEAR (Book #10)
LEFT TO PREY (Book #11)
LEFT TO LURE (Book #12)
LEFT TO CRAVE (Book #13)

THE AU PAIR SERIES
ALMOST GONE (Book#1)
ALMOST LOST (Book #2)
ALMOST DEAD (Book #3)

ZOE PRIME MYSTERY SERIES
FACE OF DEATH (Book#1)
FACE OF MURDER (Book #2)
FACE OF FEAR (Book #3)
FACE OF MADNESS (Book #4)

BEFORE HE ENVIES (Book #12)
BEFORE HE STALKS (Book #13)
BEFORE HE HARMS (Book #14)

AVERY BLACK MYSTERY SERIES
CAUSE TO KILL (Book #1)
CAUSE TO RUN (Book #2)
CAUSE TO HIDE (Book #3)
CAUSE TO FEAR (Book #4)
CAUSE TO SAVE (Book #5)
CAUSE TO DREAD (Book #6)

KERI LOCKE MYSTERY SERIES
A TRACE OF DEATH (Book #1)
A TRACE OF MURDER (Book #2)
A TRACE OF VICE (Book #3)
A TRACE OF CRIME (Book #4)
A TRACE OF HOPE (Book #5)

CHAPTER ONE

Rosa stood on the side of the road, her back to Santa Domingo de Silos, the site of the revered medieval abbey. Northern Spain could be warm this time of year, so she stood beneath sparse tree cover, with the faint hint of thick air rising on the wind. Now, below the Burgos Province, she was running out of options.

Her thumb jutted beneath the summer sky, one hand on her hip as another vehicle pulled past, ignoring her.

She frowned at the fleeing sedan, the angry red taillights meeting a glare of her own.

"Mierda," she muttered beneath her breath. She'd thought by coming to one of the more popular pilgrimage sites she'd have ample opportunity for transportation. She needed to reach Madrid. Her sister had offered her a room for the next two weeks.

This could be it… a chance to reconcile.

Her shoulders stiffened slightly and she reached into her pocket with her free hand. The other maintained the wavering thumb over the dusty road. The sound of birds chirped from the sparse trees, flitting against a backdrop of some postcard, the stone-structured, medieval abbey visible over the curve of the switchback.

Her scrambling fingers withdrew her emaciated wallet. She flipped it open, if only to confirm what she already knew.

Empty.

Not even enough for bus fare or a bribe.

She felt a familiar sense of anxiety welling up inside her, filling her with horror. But she didn't scream. She didn't shout. Rosa stood straight-postured, proud. She had to make it to Madrid.

Then her luck would change.

She took a step into the roadway. More out of insistence than any attempt to blockade traffic.

This time, a passing car leaned on its horn as it swerved around her in a cloud of dust. A man flashed a middle finger out the driver's side window, which she was more than happy to return. *"Bastardo!"* she called after him, switching the digit of her upraised hand. "St. James spits on you!" she yelled after the car.

This time, the red brake lights went on and didn't flick off. The car

1

was coming to a halt. The front door began to open and she heard a stream of cursing in Spanish.

With a yelp, Rosa turned, hastening in the opposite direction, down the small incline, beneath the twittering birds in the trees, tracing along the metal barrier protecting cars from tipping over the drop-off.

Once she was out of sight, around the bend and confident the man wasn't chasing after her, she jutted her thumb up again, her other hand on her waist, tilting her hips to accentuate them. She needed to get to Madrid. Nothing else mattered now.

She never considered herself particularly religious but many sorts who came through this way were following the path of St. James. The revered apostle. A little prayer couldn't hurt.

"Please," she murmured beneath her breath. "Help me, uh... James? And Mary. Yes. Help..." She nodded her head as if in farewell and flashed her thumbs up at the clouds. She wasn't sure the etiquette of ending a prayer properly.

As she did, tilting her face to the sky, she heard the snarl of another approaching engine.

Rosa turned, sighing and not daring to even smile. So many cars had already passed by; what would be the point of getting her hopes up again? Still, she kept her arm extended. She needed to get to Madrid. One way or another. Her life would have a second chance. Her sister would give her a place to stay. She might even find an honest job. She was tired of living like this, broke all the time, moving from one bad boyfriend to the next, following promises that were never fulfilled. She'd wanted to start a family by now. She sighed, feeling a lump in her throat, wondering how things had gotten off track so quickly. Still, she was young; she had her whole life ahead of her.

This new car moving up the road was a dilapidated rust bucket. The front was streaked with weathered portions of stripped paint. The windows were low, and one of the mirrors had been replaced with the wrong color. It would have been wrong to say the car was green. More like, it attempted to be green but failed halfway through the effort. The sun, over the course of what looked like a century, had worn the rust bucket out. Surprisingly, though, the windows were pristine. Not a visible smudge as the car slowed, drawing near. To her astonishment, the passenger side window of the old jalopy began to roll down. She peered into the window, toward the person sitting within. Her eyebrows went up. "Hello," she said, trying not to sound too eager.

"Hello," the voice from within replied. A crisp, clear tone. She had an ear for that sort of thing, given how many boyfriends she'd gone through. She could pick out a drunk a mile away. Could pick out a drug user. Could pick out someone in the throes of depression. All these things she'd experienced. This person, though, was straight-edged. She could tell instantly. The crisp, clear voice, eyes alert, posture straight. The interior of the vehicle immaculate, despite the worn exterior. The person's hair was neatly combed, not a single strand out of place.

Perhaps her prayers had been heard after all. "Are you going to Madrid?" she said, flashing as charming a smile as she could manage and jutting her hip out just a bit more. She didn't have any money, but she'd often been told she was charming.

The man seemed impervious to this, though. His tone was calm. "I can," he said. "What are you offering?"

She blinked, staring through the open window. "I'm," she said, hesitantly, "I'm sorry, but I don't have any money."

"I see. Is that why you do this? For money?"

She hesitated, wrinkling her nose. Straight-edged, perhaps, but something was off. Something in his eyes. He didn't blink. His voice was calm, soothing, but his posture was rigid, as if someone had installed a rod of iron in his spine. "Money? No, I'm not trying to get paid. I just need a ride. When I get there, I can probably help with some gas."

Inwardly she kicked herself, hoping her sister wouldn't rip her apart for the promise.

"It's a sin to sell your flesh," the man said, still softly. He shook his head, his dark eyes fixated on her now. "Do you know where we are?"

"I—yes."

"This is a gathering for pilgrims. It is not the right place to do what you're doing."

Now she felt a flash of irritation. "What do you think I'm doing?"

He waved a hand toward her hip, toward her thumb. "Offering what the good Lord gave you for free. Offering what isn't right to share with anyone. It isn't right. It is a sin."

Her mouth felt suddenly dry. "I'm..." She hesitated, studying the man, and then cursed. "I'm not a *prostitute*. What? No. I need a ride. I'm not—not doing *that*."

She would have been lying if she said she'd never considered it. She wasn't bad looking, as her slew of boyfriends could attest, but she wasn't sure she could face her sister or her nephews if she'd gone down that route. Her irritation was now turning to discomfort. The man was still watching her, not in a lewd sort of way. Another expression she was all too familiar with. Rather, he seemed to be weighing something.

3

As if passing judgment. Not an emotional, insulting sort, though. The man carried himself in a way that suggested he was weighing actual outcomes. Wondering how he ought to act next. A slow breeze came over the trees, and the birds above seemed quieter all of a sudden.

Her heart strained in her chest, and she took a step away from the car. "You know what, thanks, but I think I'm good. I'll walk."

"You're lying." His voice was still calm, not at all matching the way his hands furiously gripped the steering wheel.

"No, I'll walk. Go away."

He held up one finger, pointing it through the clean window. "A lie." He held up a second finger. "Promiscuity." He held up a third finger. "And using foul language. Haven't you heard? Do not let any unwholesome speech come from your mouth." He shook his head. "Child, you should know better."

She began to walk back in the direction of the abbey. She didn't need this shit. Who was this guy, coming along all self-righteous? She needed to get to Madrid. And she certainly didn't want to do it in his car. As she stalked back up the road, trying to distance herself, he continued to follow at a snail's pace.

"I will not drive you, but I can give you this," he said.

She hesitated, walking, but feeling a prickle up her spine. She should have just kept going. She didn't know why she didn't. But she was desperate. She needed money. She needed to get to Madrid. So she turned, slowly, still walking, but glancing through the front windshield. To her surprise, in his hand, he clutched a role of euro bills.

She went still, eyes wide. "I'm not a prostitute," she said, insistently.

"This is charity, dear. Compassion. I don't want anything from you."

She wet her lips with her tongue, feeling suddenly nervous. She needed the money. But the man was strange. He'd accused her of being a prostitute. He'd called her a sinner. Did she really want his money? Then again, hadn't that been what had gotten her into the situation? Pride? An unwillingness to accept help from her family? She sighed, swallowing her pride and extending a tentative hand toward the money. "You sure, *señor*?"

"It's the Lord's work."

She extended a hand through his window, her fingers brushing the crisp bills. The money would change a lot. It looked like a month of rent. Maybe there were still good people around, even somewhat strange ones.

4

Her fingers rested on the money and that's when his demeanor shifted. Calm, rigid, all of it suddenly faded to sudden rapid motion. His hand shot forward, snaring her wrist and yanking her forward. At the same time, his other hand hit the button to the window, and the glass started to rise toward her neck. Her head had now yanked through the window. She cursed, trying to jerk back, yelling as she did. But he held her tight, pressing the money into her hand. He gripped her halfway through the window. The glass now pressed against her arm, then slipping past, rubbing raw against her skin with a flash of heat. It hit her neck, pressing her head up, up.

"Stop!" she gasped. "Please, stop!"

He said, in the same calm, soothing voice, "The Lord sees it all. We cannot hide."

The window was now pressed tight against her throat; she was choking. It was difficult to breathe. She tried to yank her head through, but she was stuck, her chin jabbing against the glass.

"He sees it all," the man said, seething. And then he put the car in park. He turned off the vehicle. She yelled, trying to kick and scream. Why had she gone down the hill, out of sight from the abbey? Where were the other vehicles? Why wouldn't they come by when she needed them most? Panic flooded her, adrenaline racing through her system. She screamed, but he ignored the sound, reaching toward the door handle and opening it.

He shoved, sending her shuffling back, kicking up dust on the side of the road as she moved with the door, helpless, her head trapped.

"Please," she said, sobbing, "please don't hurt me. I'm not a prostitute. Please!"

He slipped from the front seat, moving behind her, out of sight now. What was he going to do? She'd heard stories like this. Was he going to rape her? She felt a chill at the thought. She should have been more careful. Should have waited or asked her sister to send money so she could travel to Madrid.

She was sobbing now, tears streaking down her cheek, one staining his pristine window. "Please," she said, her fingers scrambling against the metal frame.

One of his hands snatched her wrist, bending it back. "Don't smudge," he snapped.

His breath was hot against her ear, and her screaming was replaced by choking sobs, the window so tight to her neck she felt like it was spraining something. Whatever he wanted, she hoped he would make it quick. It wouldn't have been the first time a man had taken her body by force.

Now he was out of sight. She couldn't turn to look at him. He was standing directly behind her. She felt his hand on her shoulder. She yelped, trying to swipe back. She tried to kick, but suddenly his body pressed against her.

"The Lord was watching and you have been found wanting. There is no redemption for those who continue in the error of their ways. You must pay."

Something sharp suddenly pressed against her neck. The sharp thing gouged deep. She tried to fight it, but she was trapped. One of her arms bent behind her back, the rest of her pressed hard against the metal. The door slammed as she was shoved toward the car again.

"Please," she said, desperate. "Please, don't."

But her pleas fell on deaf ears. The sharp sensation against her neck suddenly felt like fire. Something hot and warm began to spew down her throat. She choked, unable to shout. Pain like she'd never felt before accompanied the sensation of his body against her from behind, holding her still. The window gripping her neck, preventing her from moving.

Dark spots danced across her vision.

"Three sins," the man murmured in her ear. But even this sound was fading now. She could barely hear him. She felt the man pushing something into her pocket, and heard the crinkle of euro notes. The money. He was giving it to her. Even as she died, the man paid her.

CHAPTER TWO

Adele watched where the Sergeant sat by the window in her small apartment, glued to the tiny black-and-white TV he'd managed to barter from the landlord.

"He really likes that thing," a voice murmured in her ear.

She glanced back toward where Agent John Renee was standing by the stove, a spatula in one hand, the scent of green peppers and onions lingering on the air.

She smiled at the tall man. "No pickles this time, I hope."

John pressed a hand to his chest and opened his mouth in mock surprise. "Pickles? From me? No, no, American Princess, only the best for you and the TV-watcher."

Adele glanced at Renee, trying not to smile. She still needed to keep him on his toes, and though she was hesitant to admit it, things were going well between them. Not just with John, but also with the aforementioned TV-watcher. Her father was now pounding his fist against the windowsill in excitement, pausing only long enough to wince, rubbing his hand.

"Is he still recovering?" John dropped his voice, his tone turning from light-hearted to concerned.

"Yeah," she said, just as softly, not wanting to attract the attention of the Sergeant. "He's recuperated mostly—it's only been a month since the attack, though. I'm just glad he agreed to come stay for a bit. And I know he likes your eggs. Thanks again… You really don't have to keep coming over just to make breakfast."

John snorted. Still whispering, he said, "If you think I'm coming over simply to help take care of your father, then you're not half the investigator I assumed. As for the eggs, if I remember correctly, last time he called them *suitably adequate*."

"Trust me, from him that's a five-star review."

John hid a smirk, returning his attention to the food on the stove, spatula clutched tightly in one hand. He went to work, and Adele turned to her father, grabbing a beer from the fridge to place on the nightstand at his elbow. Already, he'd drained two. It wasn't even ten in the morning. Then again, things were going so well between them, Adele decided she had to pick her battles.

At that moment, John's phone began to ring. He glanced at the device, then quickly turned it off, flashing Adele a quick smile. She returned the expression, though her gaze flicked to the phone.

Adele liked to think she was learning not to ruin contentment with a sense of foreboding. It would have been a lie to suggest she'd had an easy life. Too many graveyards carried headstones to the contrary, but now, standing in her small apartment in the heart of Paris, in the same complex where she had once lived with her mother, Adele felt a sense of contentment.

She couldn't choose the people she loved. At least not always. Her father, with his walrus mustache, thick, sailor arms, and white T-shirts stained with mushroom soup cut an amusing figure where he pounded a hand while watching reruns of a soccer match. John, now more than a friend, had softened around the edges a bit. He was still the cantankerous, grumpy agent, but not around her as much. He seemed to trust her, letting her in. Standing there, she felt an odd tingle of warmth in her stomach.

At that moment, she heard a sizzle and a curse. She glanced over to see John sucking on his thumb and wiping at his eye, blinking while hastily lowering the temperature for the fried peppers. The fragrance of the food made her mouth water, and she took a seat at the kitchen table, crossing her hands. She watched as John rubbed his eye. "I survived two tours in Iraq," he snapped, "but I'm going to lose my good looks to a pan of peppers. What a tragedy."

Adele smirked. "I think you look fine."

"Keep it down, lovebirds," her father called out over the sound of his TV. A second later, the volume increased, and the faint static of the screaming soccer fans filled her unit.

As John rubbed at his eye, though, grumbling to himself, Adele's mind was tugged from the solace of her apartment. For a moment, the cold swished through her as she remembered...

A small man, also touching at his eye. A dull, unseeing eye. A man with frail bones, but quick movements.

Her stomach twisted at the memory. He hadn't resurfaced after he'd dove into the water—they hadn't found the body. Part of her suspected he was long gone. Another part of her hoped he was so injured, he wouldn't hurt anyone again. Maybe he had drowned. For now, though, he seemed to have chosen to leave her alone. She felt an odd sense of satisfaction at this which saw her hand curl on the table in front of her. She'd made the same fist her father was now slamming against the windowsill again. Maybe the two of them weren't so different after all.

8

"Dammit, sorry, I should take this," Renee said quickly. He pulled out his phone as it began to chirp again. Renee hurried around the edge of the kitchen, toward the hall which led to the bathroom. Adele frowned as he left, listening to his voice as it dropped to a whisper and he muttered into the phone.

She waited a few seconds, her frown turning to a scowl as he returned.

"Who was that?" she said.

He looked at her innocently. "Wrong number. I thought it was work."

She shook her head. "That's the third strange call you've gotten this week."

"You keeping count of my calls? Bah. It's nothing—just a wrong number." John gave an innocent shrug and returned his attention to the peppers.

Adele kept her hand clenched on the table. Part of her wanted to believe Renee. It wasn't any of her business, was it? She didn't want to turn into the stereotype of a nagging girlfriend. Dating someone like John always came with baggage. He was a cagey man, a dangerous one. That was partly why she enjoyed his company.

With a sigh, she got to her feet and grabbed a few plates, arranging them around the table. She began to move toward the silverware drawer, when John's phone began to ring again.

A few times now, in recent memory, he'd fielded phone calls that he'd explained in suspicious ways. Now he winced, holding up the phone and turning his back to her, blocking his mouth with his shoulder. "Hello?" he said, his voice barely a murmur.

She glared at the back of his head, waiting for him to turn around.

She didn't want to be the nagging girlfriend but she also didn't want to be the idiot girlfriend.

She waited tentatively, wondering if it would be rude to step closer to listen in. John responded in a hushed tone, followed by the faint crackle of a voice she couldn't make out. The last relationship she'd been in had ended in a surprise. She had thought she was going to get a wedding ring. Instead, Angus had broken up with her.

Adele brushed a hand through her blonde hair, crossing her arms. While Agent Renee cut an intimidating figure, standing a head and shoulders taller than most, the scar along his chin, down his neck into his chest giving him the look of a dangerous man, Adele wasn't exactly a shrinking violet. She was five-foot-nine, taller than most women and the average man. She worked out, preferring to run, a routine she observed religiously, waking up at five and getting in a good two hours before the day demanded her attention.

Now, as she studied John, she refused to back down. As he lowered the phone, she said, firmly, "All right, big guy, who was that? And no, don't dodge."

John looked at her, wrinkling his nose. He scratched at the underside of his chin, his neatly gelled hair brushed to the side with only a single strand loose against his forehead, like a Superman curl. "Work," he said. "They need us in, right away."

He turned off the stove, grabbed a handful of peppers, hot, as if to prove some sort of macho point, and tossed them in his mouth. Then, with the same hand he'd touched the greasy vegetables with, he patted her on the shoulder and stalked toward the door.

Adele gaped, turning after him. She felt stupid. Why couldn't she just trust him? He had been receiving strange phone calls, but maybe her own suspicions were getting ahead of her. She felt a slight jolt of guilt as she said, "Right now?"

"Yes. Now. That's what they said."

"A case?"

John was already pulling on his shoes, nodding his head while wiping his greasy hand off on his pants. "I'm guessing it's not a birthday party. I'll drive."

"Of course you will," she muttered beneath her breath. Adele sighed, double-checking the stove was turned off. "Dad," she called, "I'm going to take some eggs to go; the rest is all yours. Mind putting the extras in the fridge when you're done?"

Her father raised a hand toward the ceiling, his thumb parallel to the floor.

"You okay? Need anything else?"

"Another beer."

Adele wrinkled her nose. "You can get that yourself. Have a nice day. I'll call you if anything else comes up. You have my number, right?"

Joseph Sharp turned in the chair, glowering at his daughter. He wagged his head, his bushy eyebrows dancing up and down almost comically. "I'm fine, Adele. Go do your job."

There was nothing more like her father than this last sentence. He wasn't high on affection, but when it came to dutifulness there were few better.

Adele sighed, feeling silly that she'd called John out, feeling uncomfortable that she hadn't hidden the beer from her father. Still, as she hastened to the stove to grab a plate of eggs and toast, she wondered what was so urgent.

She glanced at her phone, noticing she'd left it on silent before clicking it back on. Two missed calls. Both from work.

Once she grabbed the eggs and took a bite, mouth full, she raced back to the door, which John kept half ajar, waiting patiently for her.

Maybe another case would be nice. Another case would help distract her from the small man with the dull eye. Another case would give her a chance to let her father have some time to himself. While she enjoyed the company, it was also nice to be on the hunt once again.

CHAPTER THREE

Adele tapped her foot nervously against the floor in Executive Foucault's office. She glanced around the room and then at the small window behind the desk. The window was closed. The normal wreath of smoke was absent from the room. In fact, the executive himself was absent.

Now, the person sitting behind the large, oak desk was the cause of Adele's rapidly tapping foot. She fidgeted nervously, rubbing her thumb across the inside of her palm as she stared in the direction of Agent Sophie Paige.

John leaned back in the chair at her side, far more at ease. His long legs stretched in front of him, one boot resting against the top of the oak table. Sophie glanced at the shoe but sighed, ignoring it, looking over the laptop lid at both of them.

"Thank you for coming so quickly," said Agent Paige. She had pinched features and neat, silver hair, without a single strand out of place. She smelled of soap, but nothing flowery or ostentatious. She didn't wear makeup and preferred sweaters to suits. In Adele's assessment, she looked a bit like a stern substitute teacher, or a nun.

Though, of course she would never say this to Paige. The two of them had somewhat of a history. They had worked cases before together. But things between them had never completely mended.

"Sorry," Adele said, hesitantly, "but where's the executive?"

Sophie lowered the lid of the laptop, the blue glow from the screen emanating off her chin and chest. "Indisposed. I'm taking his place for the morning. He'll be back later."

"Is he all right?" Renee said, his tone more curious than concerned.

"Foucault is fine," Paige said, crisply. "Could one of you close the door."

Adele glanced back, realizing in her surprise at seeing who was sitting behind the desk, she had forgotten to shut the opaque glass door, which led to the hall of the third floor of the DGSI headquarters.

She sighed but got quickly to her feet, moved over, shut the door, and returned. As she settled again, Agent Paige said, "Like I said, thank you for coming quickly. We're not sure what we have, but it's a matter of concern."

John crossed his other foot over the shoe that was already resting on the oak table. Paige glanced at the feet, her eyebrows narrowing a bit, and shot John a look as if to say, *really?*

Renee just folded his arms over his chest and watched her back, as if daring her to make a big deal of it.

He was always pushing boundaries, always testing authority, and Adele could only hope John wouldn't push it too far. If there was one person she didn't want to irritate further, it was Paige. This was the sort of woman who was ruthless if crossed. Still, at least for the moment, Sophie wasn't glaring at her.

"Two bodies," Paige said, crisply, glancing at her computer screen and then looking up again. "The executive has already filled me in. First, a priest was killed in southern France in the Saint-Jean-Pied-de-Port commune a few days ago."

"A priest?" Renee said, wrinkling his nose. "What sort of person kills a priest?"

"I believe," Paige said curtly, "that's why they call us *investigators*. I need you to investigate."

Renee glared. "And the second victim?"

"Yesterday in Spain."

"Also a priest?" Adele asked.

But here, Sophie shook her head ever so slightly. Only a single back-and-forth motion before her chin went still. The sort of woman who didn't want to waste so much as a gesture. "In fact, no, not another priest. A young woman. Outside Santa Domingo De Silos in Northern Spain. She was found with her throat slit."

"So what's the connection between them?" Adele pressed. She didn't quite meet Sophie's gaze. She wasn't courageous enough to maintain eye contact for too long, but now she could feel her curiosity rising.

"Both of them had their throats cut. It's a tentative relation as it is, but the nature of the weapon is what connects them." Agent Paige folded her hands primly in front of her, and in an impassive tone said, "Calcium carbonate was found in both wounds. Both victims were killed with an unusual weapon."

"Let me guess," Renee said, grunting, "we don't have a clue what the weapon is."

"Not yet. Some think it might be a bone or some sort of geological construction. We're not sure. But it's odd enough and close enough proximity in both time and geography that the executive thinks it prudent to send a couple of agents to investigate."

13

Adele nodded hesitantly. "Is that all we know? They were killed by a strange weapon, their throats slit? Are they related in any way? Was the woman religious?"

"It's not clear as of yet but it doesn't seem like they have much of a connection. I'll be sending you their files, and you can make whatever deductions you deem appropriate. My only question, Agent Sharp, is if you feel up to the task."

Adele frowned, but just as quickly hid the expression. "Excuse me?"

"I know things have been difficult for you over the last few months. I didn't want to put undue pressure. I mentioned to the executive that perhaps it would be best for him to assign someone else. But he said I ought to give you the option." Sophie sounded disappointed for a moment and Adele resisted the urge to glare.

"I'm fine," Adele said, lips tight. "Thanks."

Sophie nodded and then added, "I'm glad. I'm here to help. The executive wants me to keep an eye on the case. I also, for the sake of department cohesion, am going to be doing performance reviews of field agents."

John and Adele shared a look. John slowly lowered his feet from the desk. "Reviews?" he said.

Paige waved a hand airily—another single gesture before lowering it again. "I'm sure you'll both be fine. But, Agent Sharp, given your interaction with a suspect of interest last month, we simply want to make sure you're doing all right. I'm here to help in any way I can."

Adele wasn't so stupid she didn't recognize a trap when she saw it. Any hint of vulnerability, any whiff of weakness, and it would go right into Sophie's report. A *suspect*, that's what he was being called. The man who had murdered her mother, who had murdered Robert, who had attacked her father.

Regardless, the *suspect* couldn't be allowed to control her life. She doubted it would give Agent Paige anything short of satisfaction to take Adele off the case. Maybe even to put her on paid leave. Adele had hoped by working together a few times, the animosity between them might have dwindled. But Agent Paige had always been ambitious. The executive trusted her enough to put her in charge in his absence. And now, it seemed, she was seizing more and more influence for herself.

Still, Adele couldn't show she was rattled. "I'm happy for the oversight," Adele said. "We could all use the help, I'm sure."

"Do you find you usually need help in the field?" Sophie said, lifting her computer lid and putting her hands to the keyboard as if ready to type.

"No, that's not what I meant," Adele said quickly. "I'm just grateful to be working as a team."

Sophie frowned, lowering the lid again, but nodded. "Well, the two of you have a flight booked in the next hour."

"Where are we headed?" John said. "France or Spain?"

"The commune first," Paige replied. "And in light of my overview, I'd like to receive regular status reports every evening. I don't put my youngest to bed until eight, so if you can please make sure you call after…"

She bobbed her head and then returned her attention to the computer, effectively cutting off the two agents. Adele got stiffly to her feet, and John followed, the two of them shuffling out of the office through the opaque door. They moved into the hall, their feet padding against the carpeted ground as they arrowed toward the elevators. Once they were out of earshot, Adele growled beneath her breath, "Overview my ass. She wants my job."

"You're paranoid," Renee said. "She's just a choir girl. The sort of student who asked the teacher to assign homework."

"She doesn't like me, John; she's making trouble."

Agent Renee patted her on the shoulder. "You don't have anything to worry about. You've got the best closure rate in the department. Even if she's trying to make waves, she's not gonna get so much as a splash. Anyway, I haven't been to a commune before."

"A religious one at that," Adele returned. "I'm going to be surprised if you don't burn up walking in."

John nodded. "Maybe I should say a prayer or two beforehand."

Adele snorted, shaking her head as the elevator doors *dinged* shut.

The connection between the victims seemed tentative at best. But it was all they had to go on. And now, with the added addition of oversight from Agent Paige, Adele would have to stay attentive, focused. She sighed as the elevator began to shake and rattle, carrying them toward the ground floor. Even the flight, in an hour, was cutting it close. Maybe she was just jaded, but again, Adele wondered if Sophie was intentionally making things difficult. For the sake of her job, Adele would have to make sure she solved this case quickly, without a fuss. The longer she took, the more opportunities it would give Sophie to cause trouble.

And as far as Adele was concerned, she had more than enough of her own to deal with.

John snored next to her as Adele cycled through her phone, scanning the case files on the two victims. Agent Renee had an uncanny ability to sleep anywhere. Now, his head rolling to the side, drool trickling down his cheek, his snores were irritating a couple of the passengers across the aisle who kept angrily jamming earbuds into their ears and shooting reproachful glances at the man imitating a chainsaw.

Adele was used to John snoring at this point and ignored it. Her eyes scanned the files, glancing from one to the next. The priest, Gabriel Fernando, had been in his fifties, with a pleasant face, bordering on cherubic. He had dimples and smiling eyes, with a thin tuft of light brown hair. His commune in Southwest France was well-known and well respected. Not a single criminal record or complaint she could see. The only odd thing was he didn't have a driver's license. Then again, in a small commune, perhaps it wasn't necessary.

She cycled to the next picture, frowning. The two couldn't have been more different. Rosa Alvarez had been in her late twenties. She had dark hair and wore too much makeup. She had a record. Nothing serious, but a couple of shoplifting charges and one hit-and-run a decade ago. The woman didn't have a known address, but by the looks of things she had family in Madrid. Adele studied the young woman. Even in the picture, she could see the weight of the world weighing Rosa down. Her eyes were shrunken, her head stooped, her shoulders slumped. This was a woman who'd braved the world, fought, and lost.

Adele lowered her phone, sighing.

No connection between them. Just the calcium carbonate in the neck wounds. But no other commonality. Maybe the killer was just a psychopath. Maybe this wasn't the same person at all.

She listened to the snore emanating from the chair next to her and shifted, jabbing John in the ribs and then glancing out the window when he went quiet, sniffed a bit, and turned, facing the aisle.

The first crime scene would have to help narrow the focus. Especially since Agent Paige was looking over their shoulder. Adele glanced at her phone, staring at the small bubble in the top of the screen that had arrived within minutes of them boarding the plane. Already, Paige was looking for a status update. She would be hounding them for the rest of the case. Each day wasted would be another excuse to cause more trouble. But more importantly, each day wasted meant another possible murder.

CHAPTER FOUR

Adele remembered a trip as a child to the southwest of France near the Pyrenean foothills. She remembered the scent of the Nive River, remembered the sense of leaving the city behind her.

Things were quieter, simpler here.

The ride from the airport had passed mostly in study, comparing notes they'd found of interest. But no connections seemed to exist between the poor priest and the unfortunate young woman.

Now, close to the Ostabat at the foot of the Pyrenees, overlooked by the shadows of the rocky terrain, Adele and John emerged from their taxi on cobblestone streets of the Rue de la Citadelle. The Port St-Jacques claimed the Nive, adorned and ornamented along the shore by the many old houses and balconies overlooking the gentle waterway. Many of the buildings boasted their age in hues of pink and gray schist and sandstone.

As John and Adele moved down the cobbled streets, she glimpsed etchings over some of the buildings, inscriptions in the walls from a bygone era. One inscription touted the price of barley in the seventeen hundreds. Another offered a prayer to an unfamiliar saint.

Beyond the first port, along the sole main street, Adele noted the Gothic church which her mother had pointed out to her on that childhood excursion. The Notre-Dame-du-Bout-du-Pont also wore an ensemble of red schist, the fourteenth-century architecture standing as a crowning jewel amidst the old commune.

"Who kills a priest?" John muttered beneath his breath, echoing the same question he'd asked back in the executive's office. "Especially at a church?" he added, growling.

The two of them made their way up the cobblestone path, heading in the direction of the old, stone-strewn Gothic church. The tall building embraced the sky, steeples and slanted roofs protruding above red and pink sides, standing out against the backdrop of the mountains. The river behind them created a droning white noise, drowning out the rustling trees at the foot of the terrain.

The small commune seemed lifted off some postcard, transported in time, plucked from centuries ago and brought to that moment. But the illusion was somewhat ruined by the flashing blue and red lights of the police car parked outside the Gothic church. As they drew nearer, Adele spotted a tall man in a suit shaking a finger at a police officer and saying, "The lights can damage the windows. It will dull their colors. Please turn it off."

The officer muttered something in return, but evidently his response didn't please the man in the suit.

As John and Adele drew nearer, the suit glanced toward them, taking in their appearance with one sweeping look. This fellow had bowed legs and a large nose. Otherwise, he boasted a masculine jaw and an easy smile, which, despite his irritable words toward the cop, he directed toward Adele and John.

"Welcome," he said. "I'm afraid the church is closed for the week. My apologies. Might I recommend the chapel, you can find it—"

As he began to point down the street, Adele interjected, "We're with the DGSI."

The man hesitated, adjusting the sleeves of his neat suit. "I see. Well, perhaps you could help a soul out, then. All I need is for him to turn off the lights. It can damage the stained glass."

Adele glanced from the flashing lights of the police car to the church. "That's fine, please turn them off," she said.

The officer sighed, giving her a look, but then, at a growl from John, he turned, stomping back to his car and hitting the lights. He muttered something beneath his breath, but remained by his vehicle, preferring to slouch against the hood and then turn to face the small fence around the church.

"Who might you be?" Adele said, glancing at the smiling greeter.

"Father Paul," he said, nodding at her. "I help keep this place open and show visitors through. Sojourners and onlookers alike are welcome inside."

"*Father* Paul?" John said. He took in the man's suit and neatly pressed sleeves. "You don't look much like a priest."

The man smiled patiently. "I am sorry to disappoint. Not all of us wear robes or shave our heads. And I believe it's appropriate to look presentable when speaking with the authorities of the land. Romans tells us that."

Adele and John shared a look. Adele was pretty certain Romans was a chapter in the Bible. She was also pretty certain John didn't know what a bible was.

"Well, Father Paul," Adele said, delicately, "I hate to intrude, but we're here to examine the crime scene."

"Of course, of course." Here, the amiable man's smile diminished.

He shook his head with a weary sigh and said, "Very sad, horrible, in fact. Why anyone would want to hurt Father Fernando is baffling." He reached for the black gate, unhooking the latch with a quiet creak and pushing it open. The bars nudged gently against the wooden sawhorses, and Adele and John stepped through into the church grounds. The man led them up slab steps toward the Gothic structure. "He was a good man. Everyone loved Fernando. Everyone in town, everyone in the commune, everyone who met him. No one had a bad word to say."

He led them through the open, arching door, the slanted sides leading to a point at the top. As they entered, Adele felt small, bathed in the shadow of the dark, immaculately maintained building. It was strange to stand somewhere five hundred years old. She wondered how many people had come through these halls. The pews faced the front. Marvelous windows displayed scenes from the scriptures, illuminated in the sunlight and casting resplendent refractions of colored lights across the stone ground. A crucifix on the wall cast in bronze settled near the center of the room, and the low-hanging windows allowed even more light to stream through as if bathing the place in the vibrant glow.

Everything smelled of dust and must. Adele wondered how they kept a place like this clean without accidentally using corrosive, modern products against old, archaic structures.

The floor was rough beneath her feet. No carpeting to speak of. There, in one corner, she spotted caution tape. No painted outline on the ground. The tape itself hadn't been secured to traffic cones, but had rather been laid on the floor. A couple of books had been left, hymnals by the looks of them, holding the tape in place.

"Is that where they found the body?" Adele said, pointing.

"I'm afraid so," Paul said, nodding once. "The investigators were kind enough to amend some of your practices in order to preserve the church. But it does mark the area, I'm sorry to say."

Adele and John approached. As they did, they heard the sound of footsteps coming from behind a hall lined with pillars. A younger man emerged, wearing a smooth, brown robe. The habit swished with his motions, but he pulled up short, resting a hand against one of the wooden pews and staring at them. "I'm sorry, who are—oh, Father Paul. I'm sorry, I didn't see you there."

The men nodded at each other in greeting. "They're with DGSI," said the older man, gesturing toward the agents.

This new arrival looked a bit like a chipmunk. He had thick, chubby cheeks and bright, wide eyes with long lashes. He looked friendly, but now concern etched his countenance. "I see. Are you here about Fernando?"

Adele paused a moment, scanning the marked portion of the floor. The caution tape fluttered from the wind through the open doorway. One of the hymnals was free of dust, but the other was caked in it. The floor was clean, suggesting someone had granted permission to wipe away the blood.

"Yes, we're here investigating the murder. Who found the body?"

"That was me," said the younger man.

"We call you Father, too?" John asked.

"You can call me Brother Rudy," he said quickly. "A pleasure to meet you both."

John ignored the greeting. "When did you find him?"

Rudy crossed his arms. "It should all be in the report. I don't mean to be difficult. I'm happy to answer any other questions."

"Humor me," John said.

The man's sleeves spilled past his stomach. "Well," he said, hesitant, "it was a few days ago now. Wednesday, I believe. I came in for morning prayers and saw him lying there. Lord preserve us," he said, crossing himself. "It was so horrible. I thought he was sleeping. But then I saw the," he shivered, "the blood. I immediately called the police. They arrived quickly. We are all very grateful for that. The Lord has seen us through this trying time, and we trust he will keep watch over us even now."

"Did you see anything out of the ordinary?" questioned Adele. "Anything that stood out?"

"The blood. But I noticed he wasn't moving. I tried to help him to his feet and then saw the wound on his neck." The young man winced, closing his eyes for a second before opening them and continuing in a softer tone. "I don't know what I could've done differently. I don't know why anyone would've hurt Fernando. Everyone loved him."

John shared a look with Adele. This was the second time they'd used the same phrase. Why would anyone murder a man universally loved? Why would they hunt him in the church and cut his throat?

"There was the one thing," Rudy said, suddenly.

"Careful," cautioned Father Paul.

Rudy hesitated, clearing his throat, and began to close his mouth but Adele said quickly, "What thing?"

Rudy stammered, glancing at the older priest. "I am—I'm sure it's nothing."

"What is it?" John growled.

20

"I shouldn't have said anything. I don't mean to speak ill of the dead. Everyone liked Fernando—I did see something unusual, though."

"Rudy," said Paul, sharply, "I'm sure they know. We don't need to speak of this in the Lord's house."

"Speak of what?" Adele said.

Rudy hesitated and then, swiftly, he muttered, "The prophylactics I saw on his chest."

"What?" John said.

"Condoms," Adele replied. "He had condoms on him?"

Rudy's cheeks were red and he kept bobbing his head.

Father Paul muttered up a silent prayer, crossing himself while wearing a disapproving frown.

"Used?" Adele said.

"Lord, preserve us," Paul muttered.

Rudy gagged, making a coughing sound and shaking his head wildly. "No. Nothing like that. They were sealed. Unused. But there were three of them resting on his chest. I didn't notice them at first, because of all the blood. But while I was calling for help, I spotted them. The investigators took them when they," he coughed, "also took Gabriel."

"I see," Adele said. "As for Father Fernando, you don't know of any enemies he might've had?"

At this, both men shook their heads adamantly. "Everyone loved him," they said, in near unison. "He was one of the favorite teachers at the school—it used to be an orphanage, but he treated everyone in the school like his own children." Father Paul hesitated, then reached into his suit pocket and pulled out a small business card. He extended it and John plucked it from between his fingers.

"I am not sure we have anything else to add, Agents," the man said, carefully. "But if I think of anything, I'll be sure to let you know. And there you have my number. I tend to turn my phone on after rounds in the evening."

Adele sighed, circling the caution tape once, glancing at the neat, well-kept floors. But nothing stood out. Someone had followed the priest into the church, either late at night or early in the morning. Then they'd jumped him.

What was this business with the condoms, though? A priest breaking his vows? Or a killer sending some sort of message?

Adele touched John on the arm; he glanced down and looked her in the eyes. She gave an imperceptible nod back toward the door.

John cleared his throat. "Stick around. We might have questions.

Good day."

The two of them began to move and as they did, John murmured, "So who kills a saint then leaves condoms on their chest?"

Adele whispered back, "We should check with the coroner. Maybe he'll give us more."

***

The coroner's studio was ten miles away in the more urban setting of Saint-Palais. Adele couldn't say why, but she was glad to leave the old commune behind her. It was one thing to go back into the past to learn from history, but another thing to live in it. Also, sometimes, what she didn't understand made her uncomfortable. Now, stepping into a cold, chilled room lined with metal refrigerators, she felt a greater sense of familiarity.

Science she understood. Corpses and evidence made sense to her.

The coroner was standing near one of the slabs, a sandwich with lettuce and mayonnaise in one hand. The contents had dripped on the ground beneath the slab. The man glanced over, peering through Coke-bottle glasses in their direction. He removed his glasses, squinting, the few strands of hair remaining on his head wispy beneath the bright lights above. "Are you the ones who called?" the coroner said.

"Dr. Gascon?" John queried, stepping forward.

The man adjusted his white coat, nodding. He gesticulated with a sandwich, sending another drop of mayonnaise flying onto the body. He didn't seem to notice or care. "That's right. Are you Agent Renee? Agent Sharp?"

He glanced between the two of them. They both nodded and drew nearer. The chill air sent tremors up Adele's arm.

"Well," the coroner said, his voice creaking, "I'm not sure I can tell you much more than I gave in the report. But you caught me on my lunch break. So I don't mind visiting on old friend. He patted the arm of the cadaver, seemingly indifferent to the mayonnaise stain he wiped across the bicep.

A thin sheet covered the body up to the neck. The coroner reached up, lowering the edge of the fabric. "As you can see," he said, wiggling his finger along, tracing the cuts on the throat, "messy. Very, very messy." He took another bite of his sandwich.

Adele stared. The cold, pale face of the corpse matched the picture of Gabriel Fernando. He wasn't smiling as he had been in the picture. The cuts on his throat were jagged, ripped, rough.

"That's not the work of a professional," Adele murmured.

The coroner shook his head. "Not the work of a knife, either."

John looked away, scowling into the corner of the room, staring at a patch of darkness, if only to look at something besides the body for a moment. When he turned back, his tone was gruff. "What do you make of it?"

The old man grunted. "Maybe our guy's first kill. Not a practiced killer. Not a good weapon. Certainly, like you said, not the work of a professional. I did find a strange deposit of calcium carbonate in the wound."

Adele wrinkled her nose, also looking away from the corpse now. The bright light behind the balding coroner caused her to squint. "What do you make of that?"

"Make? Me? Nothing. It's your job to make. I just tell you what I see. The weapon wasn't a knife. Maybe bone. Maybe something else. Certainly unconventional."

"We heard the body was found with unused condoms on his chest," Adele said, carefully.

The corner scratched at his head and nodded. "I was told the same thing. I don't have those. In evidence probably."

"Could that be connected in some way?"

The coroner shrugged. "Maybe some jilted lover. You know some of the stories that come out with these sorts. Or could be something more licit."

Adele shared a look with John; they both shrugged.

"Well, anything else?"

"One other thing. No defensive wounds. Fingernails undamaged. Hands were fine. I have to reckon the poor guy didn't see his killer coming. Or maybe he knew the fella." The coroner shrugged. "That's what I have. If I find anything else, I'll let you know."

Adele and John nodded farewell, taking another long look at the hapless victim. Then, with twin sighs, they turned and began to make their way out of the studio back toward where they had parked their rented car.

"Well, that's a big dead end," Adele muttered. "He didn't tell us anything new. Our victim was killed with a weird weapon. Maybe he knew the guy. Maybe he didn't."

John returned, not speaking nearly so quietly. "If it is the killer's first victim, and this girl is his second, he's escalating fast. Normally serial killers ease into it. This guy is breaking into an all-out sprint."

Adele began to reply but then her phone buzzed. She cursed,

glancing down. Another text message from Agent Paige. "She won't leave me alone," Adele snapped. "What does she expect us to report? We just got here."

John shrugged. "Not going to connect the dots until we see the second crime scene. I haven't been to Spain in a while."

Adele wiped a hand across her forehead, which felt clammy from the short stint in the coroner's lab. "Right. You set the tickets up. I'll try to keep Agent Paige off our backs."

CHAPTER FIVE

It had been a while since he'd managed to get on a plane.

Now, the painter peered out the small window, watching the clouds. They were art in and of themselves. The beauty of the sky, and the way the sun caught the condensed vapor against a backdrop of blue seemed like some infinite canvas.

He smiled, rubbing a hand against his leg.

It had taken him a couple of weeks to recover from the dive off the bridge.

He leaned back, pressing his head against the cushioned rest, tapping his fingers against the plastic tray.

A large woman next to him was taking up too much of the armrest. There was a time, out of curiosity, he might've inquired of the woman about herself.

But he wasn't looking for another job. Not now. He knew why he was here.

The plane dipped from the sky, through the clouds, shredding the vapor with metal and engine and fuel.

He wrinkled his nose, continuing to tap his bony fingers against the tray in front of him.

His eye itched. His body ached. He'd been lucky he hadn't broken a bone by jumping into the water. His bones healed slower than most.

"First time in California?" the woman at his side whispered in his ear.

He glanced over, regarding the way her hands gripped the armrests, her knuckles white in panic.

He sniffed. "No," he said in nearly perfect English. "I have been before. First time in a while, though."

The large woman nodded her head, her double chin squishing with the motion. He studied her neck. Studied her oversized body, her engorged breasts, the way her stomach jutted past her seatbelt, and the cushions of fat protruding around it. He had an eye for the human figure. He liked to study bodies. He liked to do other things with them too.

"I'm here for work," he said, delicately, his eyes flashing. At a distance, due to his size and youthful features, people often thought of

25

him as a child. This had helped him in the past.

But now, up close, the woman must have glimpsed something in his gaze. She cleared her throat and turned to face the headrest in front of her. "Forget I asked," she said beneath her breath.

He smiled, watching the side of her chunky neck. He liked to know she felt him watching. He liked the way his gaze made her squirm. That big hefty twitch and fidget. He could've made that body do incredible things; the ecstasy of sex was nothing compared to the rapture of sheer agony. Pain could contort and twist and reform. Pain was the absolute source of truth and honesty.

And every painter had to be honest.

He glanced out the window, peering through the clouds, staring at the airport as they began to descend.

He had been telling the truth. He had been here before. And he had returned once again for work. He felt the chill air from the nozzle above against his cheeks. He pulled his sweater tight around his form, tugging at the sleeves until they hid his hands.

She wouldn't even see it coming. His true friend. The person this was all about now. He wondered how she would react when she found out. Especially given what he had in store. He was going to tell her himself. Face to face. Yes. That would be his crowning achievement. The look of shock, of horror, of grief, all of it mingled into one. And there was nothing she could do about it. He would watch. She would cry.

And then he would smile.

He was here for work. And that work had a name.

CHAPTER SIX

The short flight from western France to Northern Spain had come and gone with a sense of mounting tension, and now as their rental maneuvered through the country in view of the mountains, Adele looked out the window with something bordering a scowl. Her breath fogged the glass as they pulled along the foot of the Pyrenees. Ahead, an old abbey stood out against the natural backdrop of the treacherous terrain.

"What's this?" John muttered as he began to slow the car.

Adele looked up, eyes to the road as the tires kicked asphalt and pebbles off to the shoulder. Ahead, a police vehicle blocked their way. A Spanish officer in a dark blue cap held up a hand as they neared. A few other cars had been pulled to the side of the road, waiting patiently on the shoulder as another officer moved from vehicle to vehicle, speaking with the commuters.

Instead of pulling off the road, though, John lowered his window and continued to roll forward, tires crunching along the dusty ground.

The officer standing by the hood of his blockading vehicle frowned, a hand lowering to his belt. He raised his hand higher, snapping something in Spanish which Adele didn't understand.

"John, slow down," Adele murmured.

The tall agent, though, as he was wont do to, ignored her. He jutted a large, muscular arm out the window, making sure his imposing form was visible as he continued to roll toward the blockade.

The Spanish officer had now reached for a radio. The crackle of static filled the quiet mountain air. John raised a hand out the window in greeting as the officer gestured at his partner.

The two of them both began to approach the rolling car.

"Stop!" the officer said in strongly accented English. "*Detener!*"

"DGSI," John said, lazily, his voice reminding Adele of an alley cat. The tall Frenchman pulled his wallet from his pocket, lifting it and displaying it toward the approaching officer.

The Spaniard stopped, staring for a moment. His radio crackled again, and he replied.

Adele looked past John, ducking so she could see through the window and meet the officer's gaze. "Apologies," she said. "We're here about the murder last night."

The officer just stared blankly at her. Adele set her teeth, wishing she'd had a chance to brush up on her Spanish. But then, shooting another look toward the identification, the officer listened to what sounded like barked instructions on the other end of his radio and loosed a long sigh. He ran a hand across a sweaty brow but then gave an instruction over his shoulder.

Glowering through the window at John and Adele, the two officers returned to their cruiser. The engine growled, the lights flashing, and the vehicle was guided slowly off the road, allowing Adele and John passage through.

"About time," John muttered.

"Thanks!" Adele called out through the window. "Sorry!" she added, elbowing John in the arm.

"What?" he said. "We're on a time-sensitive case. You're the one who keeps telling me, American Princess. Well—this is me. Being sensitive. To time."

"Big old sensitive John, that's you," Adele muttered, rolling her eyes. While she was still mid-motion, John leaned in quick, pecking her on the cheek with a laugh. He returned his attention out the window, smirking. Grumpy at times, always eager to bend the rules, sometimes Adele wondered why she cared for the large man. But it wasn't hard to remember. Adele didn't need a partner who watched her emotions as if they were fragile china. John was competent, spontaneous, and unpredictable.

Adele tried to keep her frown, but found it difficult, especially given the prickle spreading along the side of her face. She sighed, leaning back and crossing her arms for good measure as John pulled them along the road, past the abbey she'd glimpsed and beneath large trees.

"You're cute when you're angry, you know," John murmured, shooting a sidelong look at her.

Further ahead, on a cleared portion of the roadside, amidst prickles and fallen branches, more vehicles were parked. These were dark-windowed sedans, without the lights. But the four men and two women moving through the scene, wearing dark suits despite the warmth of the day, were obviously law enforcement.

John pulled slowly off to the side of the road, the tires scraping over the edge of the path. As he parked, Adele was already bounding from the front seat. Two planes, a taxi, and two rentals later she was glad to be walking around again.

She moved hastily toward the crime scene, where caution tape stretched between the trees and Spanish detectives moved through the terrain.

"*Hola!*" called a woman near the edge of the road. A few of the others glanced over, but when they realized who'd spoken they continued their work, suggesting the woman had the authority to speak for the rest of them.

Adele adjusted her suit and marched toward this figure. The woman in question was very tall. Even taller than Adele. She had flat cheeks and a wide face with bright, intelligent eyes. Her shoulders were broad and her hands unmistakably feminine. She dressed in a neat suit with a trail of red flowers stenciled into the lapel, down toward her jacket pocket. She also wore very expensive-looking shoes, clearly polished.

The woman didn't seem to mind the dust, though, and she waited patiently for Adele to approach, John lagging just a bit behind.

"Hello. Interpol correspondent with DGSI," Adele said, carefully. She flashed her own credentials.

The tall woman nodded. "Ah, yes," she said with a light accent. "I am Serra Pascal."

"Adele Sharp. He's John Renee."

"Right, well, Agent Sharp, Agent Renee, on behalf of the CNI, welcome to España." The woman flashed an easygoing smile, crossing her large arms over her even larger frame, her feminine hands resting against her biceps, where the sleeves of her suit crinkled. The small thread stenciling of red flowers stood out in the shadows and folds of her thin jacket.

"Our supervising agent mentioned she'd called ahead. Were we expected?" Adele pointed back down the road. "We seem to have alarmed a couple of your officers."

Agent Pascal waved a hand airily. "Ah, no, no, it is fine. We are expecting you." Even as she said it, though, she didn't move. Instead, clearing her throat, she said, "We hear there was a similar case in France. Is this true?"

Adele hesitated but John stepped in. "How about we take a look at things here, then we can recap, hmm?"

The tall woman glanced at the even larger man. She gave him a long look, nodding once in a sort of mild approval. "Yes, of course, the CNI is more than happy to help. However, we were under the impression Spanish hospitality would be met with cooperation. We're all here to help, no?"

John frowned, but before he could take the lead, Adele interjected.

"Of course. Yes, we had a similar case near Saint-Jean-Pied-de-Port. The commonality seems to be the murder weapon."

"I see," said Agent Pascal. She began to turn now, presenting her intimidating silhouette as she faced the dusty portion of road surrounded by CNI vehicles and agents moving about the space, scattering leaves and examining portions of the trail.

"Ms. Alvarez's body was found over there, by the side of the road. One of her shoes was found there." The Spanish agent pointed back along the road, down the small incline toward a gully.

"Her shoe was found distanced from her body?" Adele said.

"It appears so."

"Was she running from our killer?" Adele scanned the area, her eyes moving from the pavement, to the metal protective barrier shielding the drop-off. The indicated space where the body was found had been cordoned off, but the victim had long since been removed. A dark patch of red stained the dirt, however, suggesting at least some of the gruesome evidence of the crime remained.

Adele moved forward and Pascal fell into step behind her. John remained back by the side of the road, frowning toward the gully, his gaze tracing the roadway.

Adele returned her attention to their host. "Our victim in France was in his fifties. A religious man—a priest."

"I see," said Pascal. "Ms. Alvarez was in her twenties. I don't believe she was religious—at least not from speaking with her boyfriend."

"She had a boyfriend?"

"*Sí.* He is waiting in the traffic line right now, in fact, where he left his car. He became... agitated when he arrived on the scene." Pascal ran a hand along her voluminous chin, but sighed, shrugging once. "I'm not sure how he knew where the crime scene was."

"News?"

"Not involved yet."

Adele snorted. "Let's see how long *that* lasts."

Pascal chuckled, wagging her head and causing the rose stencil on her suit jacket to shift. "Yes—yes, perhaps not long." She spread her fingers toward the dusty patch of cordoned trail. "Rosa's neck was slit."

"How was it done?" Adele said, carefully. "Was the cut deep? Clean?"

"I—no. The, what is the word in English... *coroner*? Yes. The coroner has not ruled yet. But initially, I saw the body. The cut was rough. Very jagged."

Adele crossed her own arms now. "I see."

"What? You look troubled."

"Nothing. Just, our guy also had a jagged cut. The killer was an amateur, we think."

"I see. A crime of opportunity, then?"

Adele didn't look at Pascal now, preferring to gaze back toward the road. For a moment she paused, thinking. Why had the woman's shoe been found separated from her body? Had she run? Had she been dragged? Why the jagged cuts? What was the killer using as a weapon? And, most importantly, what was the motive? If this really was a serial killer, why take out a French priest and then cross a country line to murder a young woman?

She'd likely been stranded, by the looks of the road. Alone. Perhaps she'd even asked the killer for help. Was it simply a crime of opportunity?

Calcium carbonate in both wounds. This had already been confirmed by Agent Paige. The same murder weapon had been used.

So it had to be the same killer, right?

But why? What did he want from a fifty-year-old priest and a twenty-eight-year-old hitchhiker? If Adele couldn't figure out what they had in common, she wouldn't be able to predict where…

Where what?

Where he struck next?

She nodded to herself, eyes narrowed. There would almost certainly be a *next*. If this was the same guy, he was killing at an astonishing rate. Two murders in three days. If… and it was still an *if*, this was the same murderer, then he was only just getting started.

Her phone buzzed in her pocket and Adele gritted her teeth, jolted from her thoughts. She growled at her pocket, not even needing to check to know Agent Paige was texting again, keeping tabs.

Of all the cases to have a nuisance looking over her shoulder, this would be one of the more frustrating.

For a moment, she considered ignoring the text. But then, with a sigh, deciding there was no sense agitating Paige further, Adele's hand began to move toward her pocket.

As it did, though, she heard a sudden commotion break out behind her.

"*Dónde!*" someone was shouting.

"No Spanish!" John barked. "English? French? No Spanish! Who are you! Stop—stop!"

Adele whirled around in time to spot a small man with spiky, gelled

31

hair desperately trying to scramble past John. The large Frenchman had him gripped with both hands around a small bicep, holding him in place. Despite his posture, John wasn't squeezing too hard, caught between a desire to protect his partner from an angry man without *hurting* said man. John was frowning, now, as the fellow continued to struggle.

The small man was kicking and shouting something fierce. "Where?" he yelled, in English now. "Where?" He rattled something off in Spanish, tears streaming down his face as he kicked at John desperately, with all his might, trying to rip free.

John winced. "Please, calm," he said, in French, in a surprisingly gentle tone. "We help. We help. Calm."

CHAPTER SEVEN

"Calm down!" John repeated, still holding the man's arm. "Hey, hey—stop kicking me. I'm warning you. Stop—" John grunted as the small, spiky-haired man scored a good one right between the legs.

John groaned, trying to yank his attacker back. But the wiry man dislodged his arm from the tall agent's grasp and began to stalk in the direction of the crime scene, tears still spilling down his face. "Please," he said in heavily accented English. He rattled something off in Spanish again

"Hello there," said Agent Pascal. "Speaking of her boyfriend…"

Adele's hand had been trailing toward her weapon. At these words, though, she lifted her fingers. "This is Ms. Alvarez's boyfriend?" she said, watching as the small man kept approaching, only ten feet away now.

Agent Pascal sighed and nodded, moving to intercept the irate young man. He was shaking his fist back toward John, his feet scuffing against the ground as he stalked forward. He continued to sob openly, gesticulating wildly at the trees with another hand. It took a second, but Adele realized he was probably on something. His eyes were bloodshot, his emotions erratic. Clearly, he wasn't thinking straight. He had just assaulted a federal officer.

John was now limping, groaning and trying to stand upright. "Adele," he groaned, concerned for the only thing that ever really seemed to bother him: Adele's safety. "Watch out!"

Adele nodded quickly toward her partner, but addressed the newcomer. "Stop!" Adele said, firmly.

Agent Pascal spoke in Spanish, holding out a hand. She spoke firmly, but gently. The man striding toward them pulled up, hesitant. He glanced off to the side, his bloodshot eyes moving wildly in their sockets. He stammered something, and Pascal murmured, "He wants to know where his girlfriend is."

"I thought you said you already spoke to him," Adele replied in English.

"I did."

Adele exhaled deeply. He was definitely on something. "Just tell him to calm down. I'm happy to talk with him."

To her credit, Agent Pascal didn't seem bothered at taking instructions. Instead of trying to shoulder into the lead, she simply nodded and translated.

The man shook his head and then pointed at Adele. He said something, and Pascal whispered, "He wants to know who you are."

The man's tears now dripped from his nose. His gelled hair seemed to be melting in the sunlight, some of the product washed by his sweat and leaving dark stains along his cheek. At first he had seemed in his early twenties, but now that he was closer, Adele glimpsed the crow's-feet around his eyes. He had a young face and wore clothing like someone just out of college, but he was older than he first appeared.

"Tell him I'm here to help find who hurt his girlfriend. In fact," Adele added, quickly, shooting a glance at the bloodstain in the dirt, "I'd actually like to ask him a couple of questions if he would give me the time."

In a gentle voice, communicating the spirit of Adele's words, Pascal translated.

John had now regained his feet and was stalking toward the small man from behind. Adele held up a halting hand, though, shooting the Frenchman a quick look; John pulled up short, waiting.

"He wants to know if his girlfriend is all right," said Pascal.

"Tell him she's not. Tell him I need his help."

After the words were translated, Rosa's boyfriend began to shake, the tears and the gel and the sweat creating a horrible mixture along his countenance. He bent over, crouching in the dirt now, placing his hand against the earth as if to steady himself.

"Please," Adele said, quietly, "I need to know if his girlfriend had any enemies. Anyone who would want to harm her."

As the question was repeated, the man began to sob again, but once Pascal finished the translation he looked up sharply. He scowled, wiping a hand along his face, blinking a few times as if seeing clearly for the first time; his bloodshot eyes bulged like marbles. Adele glimpsed a couple of tracks between his fingers that played in the dirt. Small pinpricks of blood between the digits where he had administered some needle comfort.

"He says his girlfriend was a free soul. He says she's been traveling Northern Spain the last few weeks."

Adele glanced toward Pascal. "Did you ask him if anyone wanted to harm her?"

"That's what he's saying. Apparently his girlfriend was recently in Leon hitchhiking. Someone at a bar there hit on her." Agent Pascal paused, wrinkling her nose. She rattled something off in Spanish, and this time the boyfriend returned just as quickly. He nodded adamantly, pointing at Adele and miming a swirling finger as if to say *hurry up*.

"He wants me to tell you that someone hit on his girlfriend in that bar. She didn't like the advances and left. But apparently he got angry, and when she shot him down, he followed her out of the bar."

"Who did? *He* did?"

"No. Someone else. Whoever was hitting on her in Leon."

"So someone followed her."

At this, the spiky-haired man blurted out, "Knife!" He said the word in broken English. He mimed a stabbing motion. "*Knife*," he repeated. He spoke to Pascal again in Spanish.

Pascal frowned now, her cheerful expression taking on a dark pallor. "Apparently, whoever followed Rose out of the bar pulled a knife on her, threatened her. She ran away."

Adele frowned. "Is he sure she ran away?"

As this question was translated, the small man became irate. He scooped up a handful of dust and chucked it toward Adele's feet, rattling something off in fury. His hands bunched at his side, and now John did step forward, gripping the man's wrist and trying to pull him back from Adele.

"Hang on," Adele said, "don't hurt him! That's fine." She glanced toward Pascal as John tried to calm the man. "So if someone tried to follow her out of the bar and that same person had a knife, what are the chances he might have followed her further? Leon isn't that far from here."

Agent Pascal hesitated, scratching at her chin, the stenciled rose on her lapel shifting as she crossed her arms again. Instead of repeating the question toward the irate man, she paused, heaving a long breath. A few of the other agents around them—scattered through the dust and dirt, beneath the trees on the side of the road—paused, looking in her direction as if waiting for some further directive.

"I can't be certain," Pascal said, "but it is possible perhaps she was followed."

"Can you ask him if he remembers the name of the bar in Leon?"

Before the question could be translated, though, the boyfriend yelled out, "The Little Puppet." He nodded adamantly. "The Little Puppet. Leon. The Little Puppet!"

The man jerked his hand from John's grip, rubbing at his wrist. Then, tear-streaked, stained with dust, bleary-eyed, he began to stumble back toward the road, shaking his head and muttering a series of curses

35

beneath his breath. As he left, John glared after him. Adele watched him leave, her heart going out to the man, a mixture of sympathy and frustration. She turned back toward Pascal. "We were told someone would be able to accompany us through Spain. To help with translation."

Pascal nodded. "I've worked with the French before. We can take my car. It is quite fast," she said, chuckling.

Adele hesitated. "Umm, we have a rental over on the side of the road. There, the one behind the cruiser."

Pascal nodded. "Just one moment." The large woman moved toward a skinny police officer standing by the bloodstain. Adele turned as well, rejoining John on the side of the road. "She's coming with us," Adele said. "You okay?"

John straightened, doing his best to hide a grimace, and growled, "He could've hurt you. You should've let me stop him sooner."

"I'm glad you didn't. Now we have a destination. The Little Puppet in Leon."

"I heard. A bar? I have to imagine women get hit on all the time there."

"Yes, but they don't always get followed out of the bar by a knife-wielding lunatic. Who knows. Maybe the bartender saw something."

They were moving slowly now back toward the parked sedan, giving Agent Pascal ample time to catch up.

As they moved, Adele glanced at John's hand, which kept straying toward his pocket.

"Everything okay?"

John's fingers reached imperceptibly into his pocket, pressing against something. His phone? Was that a buzz she'd heard?

"I think you might be getting a call," Adele said, innocently, resisting the urge to glare.

John just shrugged, picking up the pace and marching toward the car. "It's nothing, no one. Let's go. We need to get there before the place gets crowded."

Adele stared after her partner, still walking slowly. She wasn't sure what to make of all of this. Was she just being paranoid? Or was Renee really hiding something?

She sighed, shaking her head, deciding to let it go. She strolled up the trail, listening to the sound of rapid footfalls as Agent Pascal caught up with them.

CHAPTER EIGHT

It wasn't much to go on, but a bar in Leon was the only lead they had.

The Little Puppet was a small, cheap-smelling place in the heart of the city. They had parked, at John's insistence, in a handicapped spot. Agent Pascal hadn't protested, but now as they exited the car and moved up the curb, her lips were pursed, and her eyes narrowed. The scent of the bar wafted out from the open door, propped by a red brick. A couple of cheap umbrellas were spread over metal tables, encircling a patio with cracked flagstones. Inside, during the late afternoon, patrons were beginning to gather for the evening rush. Music blasted from inside the space.

The three agents moved into the Little Puppet and immediately found themselves surrounded by bright pink and green fairy lights arranged conspicuously along the top trim of the bar. The bar itself boasted a handful of customers, most of them playing billiards or darts. A few of them were smoking in one corner, laughing and taking turns showing each other videos on their phones.

Adele looked away, making a beeline toward the counter.

An old woman, easily in her sixties, with pale silver curls was standing behind the counter, stacking slick cups. The cups were of different colors, some purple, others red and blue. Each of the cups was matched according to color and stacked in a sort of pyramid at different sections of the counter.

Adele cleared her throat, careful not to knock over a pile of orange cups in front of her.

"Cup stacking competition isn't for another hour," the old bartender said in English, giving them a once-over, her voice hoarse.

Adele shook her head. "I'm not here about that," she said, hesitating and then waving a hand toward the pyramids of drinkware being laid out. "I'm here for information."

The woman paused, settling a maroon cup at the very pinnacle of a six-stack pyramid. She said, hesitantly, "Who are you?"

Her English was better than Adele would've thought. A lot of the larger cities in Europe had multilingual entrepreneurs. It came in hand with tourist destinations. They also had a knack for picking out

37

foreigners among locals.

"Agent Sharp; I'm with Interpol. I was wondering if you saw this girl last week." She pulled out her phone, flashing the photo of Rosa Alvarez.

The woman behind the counter shrugged, not even looking at the picture. "A lot of people come through."

"Is that a no?"

"I might remember her," said the woman, leaning back now and tapping one hand against the counter. A few of the cups shifted. "Did she do something?"

"It pertains to an ongoing investigation," Adele said. John and Pascal contented themselves to stand behind her, looking sufficiently intimidating based on size alone. John was glaring, Pascal looked curious.

"I can't say I remember her. What was her name?"

"Her name?"

The woman snapped her fingers in irritation. "Name. I'm not as good with faces as I am with names. What was her name?"

"Rosa Alvarez," Adele said.

One of the customers further down the counter was looking over, watching them curiously. The man wore a backwards cap and a thick jacket despite the warmth. He already had a half empty glass in front of him, and by the look of the stack of bills in his hand, he wasn't even close to done.

Adele looked away again and said, "Rosa Alvarez. Does the name ring any bells?"

"It does, in fact. I think I remember her. She sat over there," the bartender said. "Six or seven days ago. I don't know. I remember because she forgot to pay her tab. I'd have to check with Luis. He's not here right now."

"Luis?"

"He helps when things get busy."

"She didn't pay. That's why you remember her? Are you sure?"

The bartender shrugged. "That's all I remember."

"Was there an altercation? Do you remember anything like that?"

"An altercation?" said the bartender, wrinkling her nose. "What does that mean?"

Pascal called something out in Spanish behind Adele. The woman with the white hair suddenly nodded, her painted on eyebrows rising high. "Oh, I see. There could've been. I don't remember. I was busy."

Adele frowned. "You sure? Is there anything you recall?"

"I would tell you if there was. But no. Nothing comes to mind. Look, we have a competition starting in about half an hour. So, if you don't mind, you're going to start scaring away customers." She made a shooing motion toward the door.

Adele bristled, but before she could reply, the man at the counter who'd been watching them cleared his throat. "Come on, Martha," he said in understandable, but accented English. "You know. It was the woman who got attacked."

Martha, behind the counter, frowned, shrugging and shaking her head. She pursed her lips in a disapproving gesture.

Adele turned to face the man with the backwards cap. "You recognize her?" Adele said, turning the phone toward him.

He didn't even glance down. "I remember Rosa." He gave a little chuckle. "She shot me down. Very pretty girl. I seen her around here a few times."

"And she was here last week?"

The man nodded, hesitated, then said, in Spanish, something Adele couldn't understand. Pascal leaned in. "He says a stranger approached her, tried to make a move, and when she restricted his advances, he got angry. He threw a glass at her. Then he followed her out of the bar."

Adele could feel her pulse quickening. "You saw all this?

The man paused, then mimed drinking from a glass and said something in Spanish again.

"He says he remembers what he remembers. Not all of it is clear."

Adele sighed. "You don't happen to remember what this guy looked like, do you?"

"Stranger," said the man in English, nodding his head. "He was stranger."

"So you didn't recognize him from before?"

The man spoke, and Pascal translated, "Our friend here with the hat is here almost every night. Says he recognizes most people." Martha nodded, her lips still pursed in disapproval. Pascal continued, "He says the man who followed Rosa was a backpacker; hadn't been around before."

Adele leaned in, excited, trying to control her emotions. "And you remember what he looked like?"

"Michael," the man said, with a shrug.

Adele wrinkled her nose.

"Name Michael," the Spaniard said, taking a sip from his glass. He nodded. He pointed toward a table further down the booth. "There. Michael."

"You're sure? You know his name?" Adele turned quickly back toward the bartender. "Receipts, we need to see your receipts."

The woman looked ready to protest but Pascal said something in Spanish, flashing her own badge, and the woman behind the counter growled, but then turned and slunk away, pushing through a swinging glass door that led into the back. Adele waited, half expecting the woman to disappear.

The man next to her was miming something with his hand. He kept brushing it through his hair and fluttering his eyes. For a moment, Adele stared at him, confused. The man sighed in exasperation and said to Agent Pascal, in good enough English, but still with an incredibly thick accent, "Pretty man, too. Not just Rosa was pretty. But man was also pretty too." He continued in Spanish until Pascal nodded.

The Spanish agent said to Adele, "This Michael was well groomed. He took care of himself. Neatly dressed. It stood out in a place like this."

Adele nodded quickly. Her own mind was spinning. Why would someone like that be in a place like this? Why would someone well groomed, as he'd put it, be hunting down priests and hitchhikers? People weren't always what they seemed…

The back door suddenly opened again, swinging on ungreased hinges. Martha stalked forward, her white curls bouncing as she slapped receipts on the counter next to the cups. "Section Three," she said. "Last six days."

The pile of receipts wasn't as high as Adele had feared. Section Three consisted of two tables by the dartboard. Adele quickly began to cycle through the receipts, pulling them aside. Pascal reached in and grabbed a stack; she also began to look at the names at the top. A few moments passed. And then Adele snapped her fingers. "Here," she said, quickly. "Michael Bassols."

Pascal didn't look up immediately, siphoning through the rest of her stack, before nodding, saying, "No Michaels here."

Adele checked the last three receipts in her pile. This was the only one.

"Michael," she said, quickly, shoving the receipt toward the man on the counter. "Is this what he ordered? Two beers?"

The man in the backwards cap wrinkled his nose though, and said, "No. Not beers."

Adele's heart fell. Before the disappointment could settle, though, Martha leaned in and said, "Waters. He ordered waters. I charged him for beers. But he ordered water. He didn't want any alcohol."

Adele stared at the woman behind the counter. "So you do remember him?"

She shrugged. "Vaguely. Not much. I do remember he ordered waters, though."

Adele could feel her heart pounding. She took the receipt, lifting it. "May we borrow this?"

Martha waved her hand, gesticulating toward the door again. "Whatever gets you out of here. My busy hour is approaching. You're going to scare away the bread from my mouth."

Adele nodded and, with receipt in hand, began to move toward the door. John watched her, twitching an eyebrow. "Michael Bassols," Adele said beneath her breath as she passed him. "Now we just need to find where he is."

CHAPTER NINE

John could sense the excitement from the two women as they settled in the car again. He wasn't sure how he'd ended scrunched in the back seat, behind Agent Pascal. The large woman was driving, claiming she knew the streets better.

He glared at the back of her head, his knees jutting against the seat. Adele was too busy worrying about paltry things like solving the case to concern herself with who drove. She was shaking the receipt excitedly as Agent Pascal rattled away into her phone, one hand on the wheel, reading the name and phone number from the bill.

John crossed his arms, reaching out to roll down the window as Pascal contacted the CNI.

This whole case was annoying. John had wanted another week off. He'd enjoyed spending time at Adele's nearly every day. Occasionally she would come back to his bachelor pad in the basement of the DGSI. More often than not, though, he found himself at her place. He hadn't spent the night. That would've been uncomfortable with the Sergeant watching. But he liked her company.

Which made it all the worse that he was lying to her.

As the two women in the front seat communicated over the phone, translating the details from the receipt to the tech team, John slipped his hand into his pocket, delicately pulling out his own phone. He scanned the missed calls. Three of them. All from the same number. Dammit.

Why wouldn't she just leave him alone? Didn't she get it?

He just wished she would stop calling. But then again was that fair? He was the one who'd made the choice. He'd started it with her. And now he wanted it to end. He could only imagine how she felt.

He didn't look in Adele's direction, his stomach twisting. He sighed, resting his head back against the head rest and wishing, with everything, he hadn't made such stupid mistakes.

For a moment, his finger hovered over the missed calls, wondering if he ought to just respond.

He glanced toward Adele. She looked up from the receipt as if sensing his attention and shot a look toward him. Her eyes flicked toward his phone briefly, and her face twitched nearly imperceptibly. She recovered quickly, though, and just smiled, nodding at him. She then turned back toward Pascal, waiting for the woman to deliver any good news.

Adele didn't miss much. It was one of the reasons he liked her so much. She called him on his bullshit. But then again, Adele *didn't miss much*. It was one of the things he least liked about her. She called him on his bullshit.

He sighed, massaging the bridge of his nose and staring out the window again. Maybe he should just tell her. It would make everything easier. He wouldn't feel like he was dragging around the weight of the world. What if he told her, what then?

John hadn't lasted this long by facing his problems. He preferred running, and at the very end, if fate demanded it, fighting to the bitter end. No, he would just ignore the calls. That would be the best thing to do. He swiped the calls aside, wiping them from the phone's memory, and then shoved his device back into his pocket.

As he did, he half thought he would feel a bit better. And yet the twisting in his stomach only grew worse.

So it was with much gratitude that he heard Agent Pascal declare, "Right, he does?" She nodded quickly, staring through the window. "All right, I'll tell them. Yes, right now? Perfect. Yes, send some locals there. We're on our way."

"Did they find him?" Adele said, quickly, her eyes wide.

"Yes," Pascal replied. "A man named Michael Bassols recently checked into a campground not far from here. About thirty minutes north."

"Really?" Adele said, her eyes wide. "Does he match the description?"

"We can't confirm. But he did check in with his identification, and they're sending over the details now."

"Are the police on their way?" John growled, looking over the shoulder of the seat. Agent Pascal glanced back, nodding once. "Yes, we'll have backup."

"That's not what I'm worried about. You need to tell the locals to stay back until we get there. We don't need them trampling over the crime scene or spooking anyone."

He could feel his own heartbeat pounding. He breathed in, out, trying to calm himself. Agent Pascal flashed a thumbs-up. She put the car in gear and floored it. John jolted back, Adele gripped the armrests, and they tore through the streets of Leon, ignoring the speed limit while hastening north.

John stared wide-eyed over the seat in front of him, wondering if this was how Adele felt whenever he drove.

To her credit, as she wove in and out of traffic, Agent Pascal displayed a remarkable acuity behind the wheel.

A man named Michael Bassols was at a nearby campground. What were the odds? So close to Leon. So close to an altercation with the second victim. Still no connection at all to Father Fernando. But a start. He had seen Adele work before. Like a bloodhound with a scent, she hunted down even the smallest lead. He would follow her wherever she led. He would just have to hope he didn't hurt her in the process. His large hand covered his pocket as if shielding the device within. His stomach turned, this time having nothing to do with the rapid pace through the city streets.

***

"What did I say?" John snapped, flinging open the door and stomping through the grounds.

He could feel his cheeks heating, his anger rising. He turned back, gesticulating wildly as Agent Pascal also exited the vehicle from where she had parked in the camping lot. To her credit, she looked sufficiently sheepish, wincing and scratching at the back of her head.

"I told them to wait," she said, beneath her breath.

John growled, wheeling back around. Police were everywhere. Nearly fifteen of them that John could see moved through the campground, speaking with anyone and anything. One of the cops was even petting a dog. The chances of anyone engaged in anything illicit sticking around were next to zero.

John shook his head, clenching his fists. Some people just couldn't think tactically. "What site?" he demanded.

Adele caught up with him, shaking her head, "The registration said he was staying at the fifth campground. Open air. I think…" She hesitated, glancing at wooden signs on the edge of the trailhead.

John followed her gaze. He couldn't read Spanish. But he knew numbers. He pointed and snapped, "There. See? One through ten."

Adele followed his attention and both of them spotted the white arrow pointing off to the right at the same time. Police were still moving through the area, a group of five heading toward Camp Site Five.

John felt his temper rising as he stalked forward, following the white arrow, Adele quickly keeping pace. Agent Pascal hesitated, but then moved off toward a sergeant who was barking instructions to some of the other officers. The Spaniards could keep each other in check. John, on the other hand, had a sinking suspicion they wouldn't find anything now.

"I told you," John growled, "they needed to wait for us to get here." Adele sighed, but didn't reply. Normally, when she didn't say anything, it was either because she didn't want to bother confronting him or because she knew he was right.

They reached the campground, standing next to a couple of officers who were now picking through a small green tent. One of the officers pulled the flap back, looking inside, unzipping it the rest of the way with a quiet sound. Inside, the tent was empty. A couple of protein bar wrappers sat in a plastic bag, which had been tied off to one of the tent poles. Whoever had rented the site didn't even want to litter. A Boy Scout? Was this the sort of person who would murder two people in cold blood?

John glanced around the space, his eyes traveling over the dusty clearing and moving toward the tree line.

"You kicked over the damn hornet's nest," he snapped at one of the officers. The woman just shrugged at him, shaking her head apologetically. "*No comprendo.*"

"No comprendo, my ass," John muttered. "Amateur hour."

Adele placed her hand on his arm, trying to soothe him. But John could feel his own temper rising. If he was honest, if he took a moment, he thought he might trace back some of his anger, some of his frustration, to origins entirely separate from the case. But that would've required a willingness to be honest. And John had spent a long time trying to avoid this. And so he fanned the flames of his own anger, stomping behind the tent and searching for anything else that stood out.

As John stood there, towering over the tent, something moved out of the corner of his eye. John frowned, turning ever so slightly. There, in the tree line, a face was peeping over a branch, watching them. John stiffened, not quite turning fully and pretending he hadn't noticed, continuing to glance in other directions around the trees. He moved surreptitiously toward Adele, one hand shielded by the tent while gesticulating wildly.

A second later, Adele noticed his motion and frowned in his direction.

John met her gaze and then, shielding his hand with his frame, he pointed off to the trees, jerking with his eyes in that direction.

Adele hesitated and then realized what he meant and looked over.

A second later, John heard a curse followed by the sound of

45

cracking branches and retreating footsteps.

They'd been made. John cursed, spinning on his heel and breaking into an all-out sprint, charging toward the trees.

The figure was now moving through the forest, heading away from the campground rapidly, breathing heavily, popping ragged gasps of air beneath the branches.

John picked up his pace, charging forward, yelling, "Stop!"

As he sprinted, he was glad the man didn't stop. There was something invigorating about a breakneck pace across the dusty ground, beneath branches, ripping through leaves and boughs, tearing through undergrowth. Even the welts from whipping branches and leaves with needles didn't deter him. John appreciated the pain. He liked the motion. He liked the chase.

His adrenaline pumped, his arms like pistons; he slammed into a toppled log, smashing it in half, the rot and mold flying.

The man ahead was lagging, struggling to make way through the undergrowth. "Stop!" John yelled.

The man looked back, his eyes wide; he let out a squeak. He was dressed in a neat suit, with combed hair. He looked a bit like a Mormon missionary.

The man cursed, trying to disentangle a velvet tie from a branch.

John could've called for him to stop again. But he'd already made up his mind. He was in the mood for a good tussle.

And by running, the man had agreed.

Adele shouted incoherently behind him. He heard other yells throughout the campsites, the sound of other footsteps making after him, but John didn't need the backup. He didn't even reach for his weapon. Instead, five paces away, he took another step and then flung himself bodily through the air, like some Olympic jumper, feeling, in that temporary moment before impact, a sense of weightlessness. It was euphoric.

The man with his tie caught in the branches managed to let out a small squeak before John slammed bodily into him, sending both of them careening into the nearest tree.

The man hit it first with a *thud*, letting loose a sound like a whoopie cushion.

John didn't even feel the pain. Only the adrenaline, the exhilaration.

Their bodies hit the ground with John on top, holding the backpacker down.

"Stop moving!" he yelled. "Stop it!"

The man let out another whimper, like a leaking balloon, and then went still.

CHAPTER TEN

The father tapped his fingers against the small cotton handkerchief he'd rested against the handlebars of his new vehicle. The rental car was now gone—he couldn't travel in it anymore. The origin of his journey started in Northern Spain, and it was permitted to reach there by vehicle, but once the journey started?

The Lord judged those who used motor vehicles.

Wind ushered across his form, ruffling his neatly combed hair. The man readjusted the handkerchief trapped beneath his palm, careful not to let it flit away from the motion of his bicycle up the back roads he navigated outside Burgos, within sight of the Picos de Europa.

Northern Spain was lovely this time of year, the glimmer of the sun above warming where his hand rested. The handkerchief prevented smudging the handlebars. He liked keeping things immaculate. The cotton fabric fluttered on either side of his hand from the breeze. For a moment, white cloth fluttering, it looked as if he'd trapped a butterfly beneath his fingers, holding it in place with sheer will. He glanced from his fingernails, across his well-lotioned hands to the flapping cloth, eyes alert and attentive.

If he released the cloth, it would fly away—making him a litterer. If he stowed the handkerchief, though, then his fingers would smudge the handlebars, making him neglectful.

He sighed now, removing his hand and slowing his pedal speed, taking a momentary respite. He removed the handkerchief, his other hand tightening on the bars, guiding his bicycle up the back roads. He folded the cloth as best he could and slipped it in his pocket. Then he gritted his teeth, angling toward a split in the road.

Both paths would eventually reach the required destination. One went up, through mountainous terrain, the other went downwards, an easy, sloping route.

It was warm outside. He'd been enjoying the breeze.

But perhaps too much. Too much pleasure.

He jerked his handlebars toward the more difficult terrain, increasing the gear on the bike until his legs began to ache. He would sweat, it would be uncomfortable, but this was the price of penance.

Absolution came costly.

Most of the Lord's errant sheep didn't understand this. Not the old priest back in France, nor the young prostitute on the side of the road. They had received their judgment in due course. He had simply been the instrument of the Lord's will—an honor leading to his own absolution.

The heat of the sun seemed to be rising now, and he could feel the faint trickle of sweat beginning to form along his brow, under his armpits. He sat straight-backed, eyes forward, expression impassive as his legs pumped like pistons—up, down, up down, pain—pain.

And yet he couldn't shake the rising sense of giddy delight at it all.

He was on a sojourn of his own. And soon... very, very soon, he would reach the ultimate destination. That was where it would all matter most.

His hands fidgeted against the handlebars, gripping the leather tight. He wrinkled his nose, remembering the way the old priest had smiled when he'd entered the church. The man had seemed friendly enough at first, but then, when he'd gotten too close, the priest had touched the man's shoulder.

When he'd reacted in a rage, the priest had seemed surprised, babbling an excuse, suggesting he hadn't meant anything by it, but had simply been trying to be friendly.

A lie, of course.

He could tell the priest was lying.

A homosexual. That's what he'd been. And he'd been making an advance. It all started with a shoulder touch and then it moved to the bedroom. The Lord watched it all. If an eye caused someone to sin, one ought to gouge it out.

The condoms he'd confiscated from a young pilgrim and his girlfriend. He'd scared the boy, but had decided to leave him alive. The age of accountability hadn't been reached in that case.

He'd looked for the best place to discard the confiscated prophylactics and couldn't think of a more appropriate disposal site than the piece of trash under the Lord's judgment. The homosexual had suffered the due penalty for his sins.

Same with the whore who'd tried to solicit him on the roadside.

He lowered his head now, gasping louder, sweat streaking down the side of his face, his legs protesting the rapid motion. The Lord didn't care about his pain. No... No, he needed to go—faster, faster, faster!

Now, he groaned with each press of the pedal, trying to stand upright on his bike as he took the steep hill.

He didn't like exacting judgment. He'd cried many a night, asking for the burden to pass from him. But would he not sup the cup of the Lord's offering? How could he dare refuse? King David had been a warrior, hadn't he? The prophets had declared the exacting judgment— the falling of violence like a scything blade.

No—no, he didn't enjoy it. Not at all. Not one little bit. This wasn't about him. This wasn't about his desires. This wasn't about his wants or his judgments.

No. Of course not.

This was about the Lord.

And it would continue to be so. He would just play the small, humble role he'd been given in it all. As long as the signs kept coming, he was determined to see them through.

To obey.

Not for his own pleasure. Not for his own means or satisfaction.

But simply out of a desire to do what was right.

CHAPTER ELEVEN

Adele tried not to stare at the man's velvet tie where he sat across from her at the local precinct.

John, every now and then, would glance up, rub his knuckles, then snicker.

Michael Bassols, for his part, simply sniffed, readjusting his position in the metal chair and refusing to glance at his ripped tie. The neat, silky-smooth item had torn in half, most of the cloth now back in the campgrounds somewhere, claimed by a tree as its spoils of war. The rest of the fellow didn't look much better. His suit was stained in mud and dirt and a few droplets of blood. His nose, which had been bleeding, had two small pieces of cotton jutting from each nostril. A twig had buried into his cheek, but was removed now, replaced by a tan patch of bandage.

John, sitting next to Adele on the other side of the interrogation room table, leaned in again, glanced at Michael Bassols, and let out another snickering laugh.

The suspect glared, folding his hands where they were cuffed in front of him.

"We can remove those if you'd like," Adele said, carefully, deciding perhaps they needed to establish some sort of rapport. She waved a hand at the cuffs.

The man shook his wrists, causing them to jangle. "It's the least you could do," he said in perfect French, his voice nasally and congested thanks to the cotton jammed in each nostril.

"What was that?" John said, leaning in and grinning again.

Adele kicked her partner beneath the table and his smile slipped a bit.

"It's the least you could do!" the man repeated, louder, but the increased volume only made his congestion more obvious, creating a sort of buzzing, trumpeting sound behind every other word.

John shook his head, clapping a hand against the same leg Adele had just kicked. He coughed, staring at the table, very thinly disguising the way his shoulders were now shaking with mirth. The big Frenchman had bruised his own knuckles and had a black eye from where Michael's elbow had caught him.

51

Adele still felt the residue of horror at the image of John Renee flying through the air, arms outstretched, two hundred and fifty pounds of muscle and adrenaline launching toward the small, hapless form of their suspect. The backpacker hadn't stood a chance. It had been like watching a leaf in a tornado.

Still, it didn't give John permission to act like a grade school boy.

"Well?" the nasally voice piped in again. "Remove them!" He shook his wrists, causing another jangle.

John, though, sobered a bit and snapped, "Nah, don't think so."

Adele looked at her partner, but John didn't look back. Instead, the Frenchman pointed a finger at the man across from them.

"You like it when you're in charge, yes? When you're in control. This is why you threaten women with knives for sex? Hmm? Well— you are not in control here, are you, little man? Do you feel in control, Michael?"

The man stared bug-eyed, his half-torn tie not so comical anymore at this tirade. He stammered a moment, eyes glassy as he shook his head. "What? No—no, I am not. What—what?" he repeated, a few too many times, clearly trying to gather his thoughts. "I did not..." He hesitated, pausing and frowning. Then, continuing in French, he declared, "I did not threaten anyone with a knife!"

"You were seen," John said, scowling. "At the Little Puppet—know that bar?"

The man shook his head far too quickly, letting out a soft squeak. "No—no, of course not. I've never been there. I don't know what that is."

"See," Adele said, interjecting, "now we know that's a lie. We have your information on a receipt there. We also had an eyewitness."

Michael's eyes bugged. He coughed, regrouping, then blurted, "Oh! Oh, the *Little Puppet*, yes... Of course. I was there. I forgot. I was so... so drunk."

"They said you ordered water," Adele pressed, scowling more deeply now and allowing her displeasure to become apparent.

"I—I don't remember," the man said, leaning back and moaning. "I just... just don't remember."

"You speak French very well," she said. "How come?"

The man shrugged. "French mother. Spanish father. We do share a border, in case you hadn't noticed."

"A border," John said, "where passports aren't usually required for EU citizens, hmm? Convenient we don't have any way of tracking your comings and goings."

Now the man in the half-torn tie looked confused. He shook his head, his small chin wagging back and forth. "No... Why would you need to? I already said I was at the Little Puppet."

"You said you weren't. Then you changed your story." John tapped his fingers against the metal table, drumming loudly. It sounded like thick raindrops against a tin roof.

The smaller man stared at John's large hand.

"How come you ran, Michael?" Adele pressed, using the momentary intimidation to catch him off guard. "How come you tried to avoid us?"

He sighed again, puffing a breath. "I... I just..."

"One moment," John said, holding up a finger. "May I help you? Please, hmm?" When the suspect didn't reply, John nodded politely in gratitude and continued, "If you continue lying to us—I'm going to probably hurt you again. I shouldn't. She wouldn't want me too. But I have a thing about knife-wielding rapists..." He shrugged, still tapping his fingers nonchalantly against the table. "Call it a pet peeve. I admit it. Sometimes, when I see a spider—I squish it." He shrugged. "I don't know why. I just don't like spiders. Is it nice? Perhaps not. But I squish spiders. Understand me?"

The man had turned pale, causing the remaining streaks of blood against his skin to stand out like stains of crimson.

Adele sighed, hoping John was only bluffing, but pressing all the same. "Why did you run, Michael? This knife of yours—we didn't find it on you. Why is that?"

The man still looked panicked, shooting horrified looks at John Renee. At this comment, though, he paused momentarily, shooting a different look toward Adele. "Wait—wait, my knife? I never used this knife... What are you implying?" His eyes widened in panic. "Did that bitch say I cut her? I didn't cut her at all! I just showed it to her. I thought she'd like it."

"You showed a woman you followed from the bar your knife?" Adele said, her voice deadpan. "That's your story?"

He licked his lips, shooting shifty-eyed glances one way then the other.

John, bored and impatient, got to his feet, snorting in disgust. "Wasting my time, Adele. I'm going outside for a smoke. Just book him for the murders. It's him. Let's go home."

Now, though, the pale-faced man impersonated a snowdrift, the blood completely leaving his cheeks. He gaped like a landed trout, sputtering a series of sounds somewhere between syllables and gasps.

At last, gathering himself, in one long, wheezing breath, he said, "*Murders?* I didn't kill anyone! I didn't kill her. I just had some fun. That was all! She liked it! She liked me… I could tell. She was hitting on me back in the Little Puppet. You should have seen the way she kept walking past my table, wiggling that cute little ass of hers. She wanted it. I knew she did. You weren't there—you don't get how women are…" He looked at John imploringly, but at a glimpse of the Frenchman's glare, he looked at Adele instead, his expression pleading.

"What do you mean you had some fun?" Adele said, her own tone going cold.

He winced, trying to hold up his hands in protest, but then realizing they were cuffed. "You don't get it," he said. "It isn't like that. She wanted it."

"Are you admitting to raping our murder victim?" said Adele.

Now the man crumbled, slumping so low in his chair, his chin barely passed the top of the table. "She's the one who is dead? I didn't kill her! I didn't! I ran because I thought you found out I'd followed her from the bar into that alley. I—I thought…" He swallowed, desperately looking around.

"Murders. Both," John said, coldly. "He did it. Put him away for the rest of his rotten life."

"No! No! I didn't kill anyone. My knife is hidden beneath a tree back at the campground. You can look at it. It won't have any blood— anything. I know because I didn't kill anyone."

"So you ran because you thought we were there about your rape?" Adele said, still cold.

"It wasn't a—a—"

"Rape," John returned.

The pale man turned, snarling. "It wasn't!" he howled, a hidden rage bursting to the surface now. He shook his head violently. "She wanted it. We both had fun. Ask her!"

"She's dead," John said. "Because you killed her."

"No—no," he moaned, lowering his head and pressing it against his cuffed hands. "It wasn't like that. It wasn't…"

"Where were you the last three nights?" Adele said, frowning.

Here, the man perked up. "Wait—three nights? That's when this happened. Great!" he said, excited all of a sudden. "Wonderful. My phone… my phone. You took it. The big one has it. Look through my phone. I have pictures from the last three nights. I was out clubbing— each time."

"Clubbing?" John snapped. He fished into his pocket, pulling out a

54

large, sleek phone. He held it across the table, jamming it toward the whimpering suspect.

Before the fellow could react, John reached down, grabbed the man's finger, yanking it so hard Adele was worried he might break it before pressing the digit against the finger-scanning slot on the back of the device.

Then, once the phone was unlocked, John straightened again. He began sifting through the pictures, snorting as he did. "Strip clubs?" he said, shooting a look toward the slumped fellow. "Three nights in a row, hmm? Classy."

"Hey, man," snapped Michael. "It gets lonely traveling for work weeks at a time. A guy has to do what he has to do."

"I wonder if Rosa feels that way," John muttered, his sneer twisting his lips as he continued cycling through the phone. As he did, though, he sighed, jamming the device toward Adele.

"All three nights," John muttered. "That's the little runt, his head buried between those silicone heavies."

Adele wrinkled her nose as John showed a slew of pictures. She clicked the device, inwardly reminding herself to wash her hands vigorously when they left, scanning the information on the picture.

"From seven p.m...." She scrolled to the final picture. "Until past midnight. Each night?" She looked at the man, eyebrows high. "That's what you do in your evenings?"

The man just glared at them now, shaking his head. "It proves I didn't do it, though. Right? I didn't kill anyone. I didn't!"

John pointed the phone angrily toward the fellow. "If any of these prove to be staged, you better believe I'm coming after you. Hard. And don't think I won't send someone to retrieve that knife of yours." John slammed the phone back on the table with a loud *crack*.

"Hey! You'll break it!" Michael protested.

"Well... you'll find out in a decade or so," John snorted.

"W—what? I didn't kill anyone."

"Guess what," John said, his tone like ice. "Sexual assault is a crime. Sit tight, Michael. Not that you have a choice."

With another disdainful glance, John pushed to his feet, gesturing Adele should follow. She glanced at Mr. Bassols's phone a moment longer but sighed.

The dates did check out. Michael himself was in a few of the pictures—not to mention, he seemed genuinely surprised.

As Adele followed John out of the interrogation room, stepping into the hall, the door behind them creaking on poorly maintained hinges as it closed slowly.

"Well?" Adele murmured, looking at John. "Thoughts?"

John scowled, crossing his arms in a way that caused his muscles to stand out more. "Wish I'd tackled him harder. We should speak with Agent Pascal and get someone to check for that knife. Someone else can comb through the pictures and interview strippers."

"Is that the sound of personal growth I hear?" Adele murmured, trying to lighten the tone. "You *don't* want to speak with strippers?"

John, though, still frowned. "We went looking for a killer and caught a creep. We still don't know where this guy is."

Adele crossed her arms, hesitating for a moment. The two of them stood in silence, outside the interrogation room, allowing their own thoughts to wander. John's seemed to only sour his temper further. For her part, Adele closed her eyes, trying to think through any possible connections the victims might have had.

If this really was a serial killer, then it couldn't be a crime of opportunity. She glanced out the large window facing the street outside the precinct. Light was now fading, evening rapidly approaching.

As the sun fell, it took Adele's spirits with it. The conversation with Michael Bassols had done little to improve her mood.

But they weren't here because of a knife-wielding pervert. They were here for a serial killer.

Were the two cases connected? That was what mattered most. The weapons used suggested yes. But the victims themselves suggested otherwise.

These could have been crimes of opportunity, perhaps. Maybe something in the interactions alone had caused the killer to lash out.

Ms. Alvarez's movements would be nearly impossible to trace. Her boyfriend had suggested she'd been all over Northern Spain. By the sound of things, she even had family in Madrid.

If tracing all her connections, all the people she might have angered or irritated or attracted, didn't end well...

So what then?

Father Fernando... His situation was different. He lived in a commune, didn't he?

Adele's eyes brightened and she began to tap a finger against her arm, shifting from foot to foot as her mind raced.

"What?" John said, his frown receding for a moment.

"Hmm?"

"Don't hmm, me. What? You look like you have to pee. Which usually means you have an idea."

"I—I do *not* look like I have to…" Adele stared, scandalized.

John smirked now, straightening, the scarred skin beneath his chin standing out in the fluorescent lights above. "I'm joking, American Princess. What are you thinking?"

Adele reached out, flicking John's wrist in retribution before saying, "It will be hard for us to track down Ms. Alvarez's movements. She's been taking buses, hitchhiking… the like."

"Right."

"But what about Father Fernando? His commune in France is fairly isolated."

John hesitated, nodding. "Yes, perhaps. So?"

"He interacts with the same people most of the time, no?"

"And?"

"Why did he die now? Why did someone else kill him? His commune is isolated. Most of the others in the commune would be conspicuously missing if they'd vanished for a few days."

"So the killer has to be a stranger, then…"

"Or someone outside the commune, yes."

"Well… A tourist?"

"Perhaps. Maybe. But if the father was targeted, it needs to be someone who knew he'd be alone in that church at that hour."

"What if it wasn't targeted—what if it was just dumb luck?"

"I was thinking about that—but don't you remember what the coroner said? No defensive wounds. If he was the only one in the church, he would heard someone arrive, surely."

"So you think he must have recognized the killer? But how does that make sense? You just said anyone missing from the commune would be conspicuous."

Adele nodded quickly. "Exactly. Which means it was someone he recognized who *wasn't* from the commune. But also someone who was in Spain only a few days later to kill again. Someone on the move, who frequents the commune in France."

"I—I don't…" John's eyes went up. "Oh."

"Right. Oh."

John said, "Even priests have to eat, no?"

Adele smiled, nodding now, glad John had reached the same conclusion she had. A delivery driver following the same route would have access to the commune—familiarity—but also not the same level of oversight. In fact, coming and going at odd hours was part of their job.

John shrugged, looking impressed. "Worth a shot, I suppose."

Adele patted the tall man's muscled forearm. "That's all I need to hear. Do you still have Father Paul's business card? What was it he'd said—we could usually get hold of him in the evening."

"No time like the present," John muttered, pulling a small, rectangular piece of paper from his pocket and handing it to Adele.

CHAPTER TWELVE

Adele waited patiently, standing on the steps outside the precinct and looking at the distant mountains of Northern Spain. The vast, blue horizon now hung heavy with darkness as evening introduced itself across the skies.

The heat of the summer slowly faded now and wafting zephyrs brought in a faint, pleasant chill.

Adele stood on the steps, leaning against a concrete support beam, listening as her phone continued to ring.

John had gone back into the precinct to grab food from the break room fridge. She hoped he wouldn't steal a local officer's pre-packaged dinner like he'd done at other stations they visited, but she wouldn't count on his self-restraint. More than once her own leftovers often vanished from her fridge without so much as a warning.

As the phone rang, she sighed in frustration when the answering machine voice began to speak.

She lowered the phone, double-checking the number on the business card John had provided. Then, determinedly, she entered the number a second time, lifting her phone once more and waiting patiently.

Two rings... four...

How late did Father Paul work?

Six...

Then silence.

Adele perked up.

A soft, crackling voice, very faint and hard to hear, spoke on the other end. "Hello? Who is this?"

"Father Paul?" Adele said, quickly, speaking louder just in case her connection was similarly poor. "Hello, can you hear me? This is Agent Sharp. I'm the—"

"DGSI, yes," said the faint voice, still crackling. "Yes, I remember. Hello, Agent Sharp. Apologies, I see I missed a call from you. I only just turned my phone back on after evening prayers."

"Yes, well," Adele said, "I appreciate you picking up. I had a question for you."

"About Father Fernando?" The man's voice sounded soft and sad now.

"I'm afraid so."

"Have you found anything, yet? Oh—look at me. Apologies. I'm not even letting you speak. Please, please, go ahead, how may I help you, Agent?"

Adele flashed a grateful smile, even though he couldn't see it. "Wonderful," she said. "Look, it isn't much. But I'm wondering who supplies your commune?"

"Supplies?"

"Groceries, Bibles, toiletries, whatever…"

"Oh… hmm… One second." The faint voice became even quieter and then Adele heard a nearly inaudible shout on the other end. "Vera! Vera—yes… Here, come here one moment. I have a question for you." A faint exchange ensued which Adele couldn't quite make out.

After a few moments, though, a new voice spoke on the other end. This fellow sounded exhausted, every word laden with a lack of sleep.

"Hello?"

"Yes? Hello, my name is Agent Sharp."

"How may I help?"

"I… I was just asking Father Paul about any supplies delivered to your commune."

"I see. Yes, well, I'm in charge of hospitality and distribution. I can probably help with that. Do you have anything specific in mind?"

"You have multiple delivery services?"

"Multiple suppliers."

"I see. Thank you, but I'm more interested in the drivers, or deliverers themselves."

"Oh. Well, in that case we get weekly deliveries by truck."

"What's the company's name?" Adele said, trying to hide her excitement.

"Passo National," said Vera on the other end, pausing to yawn before continuing in a lethargic tone. "We've been with them for four years now."

"And the deliveries are weekly? Did one come through last week?"

"I—yes… Three days ago. Why do you ask, Agent?"

"No reason. Thank you for your time. Please thank Father Paul also, I have to go."

"This isn't about the murder, is—"

Adele hung up, wincing as she did. Wondering if it was bad luck to hang up on a priest. Still, for now, it seemed, her luck was running strong. She slipped her phone back into her pocket. She turned hastily toward the precinct, moving back in the direction of Agent Pascal's temporary desk.

The tall, broad-faced woman was sitting in a space far too small for her size. As Adele approached from behind, she noted the woman was murmuring something to herself, her eyes closed, something rattling in her hand where she reclined in her cheap, plastic chair she'd been loaned by the locals.

The CNI agent continued to murmur as Adele came close. The woman's eyes fluttered for a moment, but she didn't seem to realize she now had an audience and continued murmuring beneath her breath.

With her eyes closed, her posture relaxed, Agent Pascal looked at peace. She seemed calm and after another few moments of quiet murmuring, she lifted a hand resting in her lap.

Adele realized the sound she'd heard came from Catholic prayer beads which were now circling the woman's hand.

Adele hesitated, still gripping the business card in one hand, but then cleared her throat. She waited, then, louder, cleared it again.

Agent Pascal's eyes opened suddenly; she spotted Adele and her lips stopped moving. Carefully, she stowed the beads back into her lapel pocket, near the stenciled outline of the red rose.

"Sorry," Adele said, hesitantly. "Didn't mean to interrupt."

Agent Pascal just smiled, her broad features communicating an easygoing attitude. "Agent Sharp, pleasure," she said in that faint accent of hers.

"Yeah, hello. Umm, look, I was wondering if we could get in contact with your CNI team?"

"Oh? For what?" Agent Pascal leaned forward now, a bit more eagerly.

"To look into a delivery company called Passo National," Adele rattled off. "Specifically examining delivery drivers who frequent the Saint-Jean-Pied-de-Port commune."

"Oh... I see. We have a new suspect?"

Adele shook her head. "The guy we brought in has a solid alibi for the murders. We're verifying it, but also looking at a new angle."

"All right. Give me one moment." She held up a long finger and then pulled her phone out, tapping a speed-dial number. After a moment, Adele heard a voice on the other end.

Agent Pascal said something in Spanish before glancing back at Adele. "What was the name of the company again?"

"Passo National," Adele said, tapping her foot against the floor again. Was she fishing in the dark? Or would the lead pay off? It seemed straightforward enough. Like John had said, even priests had to eat. And this way, a delivery driver would have access to the community without being noticed missing.

Pascal seemed to sense Adele's hesitation. She smiled, reaching out and patting the younger woman on the arm. "It is a good idea," she said. "I'll see what we can find."

***

Adele's arms were crossed so tightly she was beginning to sweat. John had rejoined them now, eating a slice of cold pizza which he'd sworn he'd gotten from the vending machine.

Instead of reprimanding her partner for stealing a Spanish cop's dinner, Adele was watching Agent Pascal—specifically watching the file now opening on the woman's computer.

Pascal's phone was on speaker, a faint Spanish voice chirping out, guiding their translator through the information and how to properly access it.

Pascal, despite a few failed attempts to figure out the software on the unfamiliar computer, still hadn't lost her temper. She seemed a very patient, even-keeled woman. Adele wished she could have said the same for herself.

But now, arms crossed, her foot was beating a tattoo into the ground.

"See?" John whispered in her ear, his breath smelling like pepperoni and mozzarella. "You look like you need to pee."

She shot him a venomous look, but returned her attention to Pascal, waiting on tenterhooks.

At last, the voice on the other end of the speaker said something that faintly felt like a farewell. Agent Pascal replied, "*Adios*." And then she hung up, lowering her phone and swiveling in her chair to present the computer screen.

"Passo National," she said, crisply, "run by three brothers and employing over two hundred truckers."

"How about those delivering to the commune?" Adele asked.

"Two, in fact," said Agent Pascal, pointing to a spreadsheet open on her computer. "A Gabino Lazar, and a Tomas Cannizzaro. By the looks of things, Mr. Cannizzaro is currently on vacation and has been for nearly two weeks now. He's currently in London. Passport confirmed."

"So only Gabino Lazar was on that route last week?" Adele said, eyes widening.

Agent Pascal nodded. "It seems so. And get this," she said, clicking on her screen and pulling up another file. This time, Adele didn't need an explanation to realize she was staring at someone's mugshot. A bald man with a beer gut and angry eyes was glaring at a camera. A few lines of text next to the photo identified him.

"Gabino Lazar has a record," said Pascal. "A few years ago he assaulted a hitchhiker."

Adele shared a significant look with John. "A hitchhiker, hmm? Like Ms. Alvarez."

John frowned. "Think he's escalating?"

"Very possible," said Adele.

"Not only that," Pascal continued, sounding mighty pleased with herself. Adele didn't blame the woman. This temporary expertise had come at the cost of nearly half an hour of annoyance, trying to navigate an unfamiliar computer while speaking with a software engineer on the other line who'd sounded annoyed by the call. Ever cheerful, the CNI agent said, "Passo National has routes that take him into Northern Spain also. Not just your commune in France."

Adele felt a prickle along her upper chest and cheeks. "I see," she murmured. "So Mr. Lazar has a record and has a route through the commune and into Northern Spain where Ms. Alvarez was found."

Pascal nodded, still looking quite pleased, adjusting her suit where she sat.

"Well, that just leaves the million-euro question," John murmured. "Where is Mr. Lazar right now?"

"Ah yes..." said Pascal, squinting back at the computer and clicking through a couple more files. She accidentally closed one and it took her a few minutes to figure out how to open it again. John tried to help, but ended up suggesting she simply restart the computer. After few moments of mounting irritation, Pascal finally brought the appropriate file back up. She tapped a finger on the screen.

"He is currently en route from Santander to Bilbao," she said, "see here? Less than an hour away."

"And that information is current?" Adele said.

Pascal bobbed her head. "My contact spoke with the company directly."

"So Mr. Lazar might know we're coming?" John said, frowning.

Adele just shrugged. "Well—we know where he is. I think it best we go and speak with Mr. Lazar."

Pascal was already rising to her feet. John and Adele both glanced at her curiously.

"I'll drive," she said, indifferent or unaware of their shared look. Still smiling, the tall woman began to lead them from the room, toward the precinct doors. "We can take one of the police cruisers," she called over her shoulder. "The sergeant is an old friend—he won't mind."

Adele shrugged and fell into step with John pulling up the rear. They maneuvered after Agent Pascal, out the sliding glass doors at the front of the precinct and making a beeline toward a new, sleek police cruiser sitting in a designated parking spot.

A couple of police officers, returning from an evening shift, nodded politely as they side-stepped the agents on the stairs and headed into the building.

For her part, between John and Pascal, Adele could only hope they would reach Mr. Lazar's truck in one piece, intercepting him on his route to Bilbao. Then again, sometimes it was good to have partners who observed speed limits more as suggestions than rules.

CHAPTER THIRTEEN

The man's legs were practically aching from his bike ride up the side of the mountain. A small bell dinged above his head as he stepped into the sandwich shop built on the slope of the mountain. The aromatic odor of wheat and flour and meats and cheese wafted over the protective glass case around the food. A pleasant young woman was moving through the tables carrying a silver tray, dressed in a sweater and long pants, appropriately modest. The man kept his head down, wincing as he took steps on his sore legs. He would have to recover. He was weaker than he thought. Absolution would come costly if he couldn't will himself to obey. There was no pain. No preference. Only latent obedience or nothing.

He stepped past a couple of tables, moving toward a booth at the back of the small sandwich shop. As he passed the waitress, she said, "I'll be right with you, sir." He nodded politely back, but didn't speak. The less he talked the fewer temptations. He wouldn't let the wiles of a beautiful woman entice him. He moved over to the booth, sliding in, sitting straight-backed and letting out a soft sigh of relief as his legs crumpled under him. He breathed a bit easier now, resisting the urge to slouch and relax completely.

A couple of other customers sat in the sandwich shop. An older couple reclined at one of the tables, eating a particularly noisy bag of chips. He hoped that they would see the sense in cleaning up after themselves. The man had dropped some lettuce on the ground. It would be wrong if he left it there.

Another table had a group of youngsters. Perhaps only in their teens or early twenties. Three boys, all of them laughing a bit too loudly. One of the young men had a bag of chips and two sandwiches he was already working on. He grabbed a beer bottle from the fridge to join another bottle he'd already emptied. The waitress was moving quickly between the two tables, brushing her hair behind an ear, clearly frazzled. She smiled in a strained way toward the young man, placing another sandwich in front of him.

The man waited patiently. Patience was a virtue. Tardiness was a sin. He would be patient, but if the waitress was late, there would be a comeuppance to pay.

It was only the first day of his true voyage. He felt emancipated. Never before had it seemed so sweet to sit in an unfamiliar place watching the sights and sounds and inhaling the mountain air.

He was free.

Briefly, he closed his eyes, holding a quiet conversation with his mind.

He wondered what his younger self would have said, seeing him now. There had been a time he hadn't thought he would make it past his youth. Despair had set in. A sickly, cloying sin. A lack of hope. A lack of trust.

His hand clenched on the table in front of him, his nose wrinkling in disgust as he realized just how putrid he was. He had been. The Lord hadn't left him like this. He was changing. He could feel it.

But once upon a time he hadn't seen a future that would end well. Once upon a time, there had been no hope.

He could remember his own priest, the sound of the whistling rod. The sudden flare of pain. He could remember his gasp as the rod hit again and again. "Sinner," the priest had yelled. "Sinner," he screamed.

And in his youth, the man had cried. Since then, he'd grown to appreciate penance. Appreciate the value of proper punishment in its place. And now the Lord was giving him signs of his own flock to respond to. Sometimes a sheep was so sick it had to be put down for the sake of the herd.

He nodded to himself, his hand still clenched against the table. A few smudge marks caught his attention, and he wrinkled his nose, daintily plucking a napkin from its holder and wiping the table clean until it was pristine and reflective.

"What can I get you, sir?" came the pleasant voice of the young waitress.

He looked up, watching her from beneath his dark brow. He straightened, brushing his hair completely in place with one hand, and murmured, "Water and bread, please."

The waitress hesitated, biting her lip. "What sort of sandwich?"

"Just bread, please, child. Thank you."

She stared at him for a moment and then sighed, turning on her heel back toward the counter.

He didn't watch her leave. He didn't speak further. The less he talked, the less he would be tempted. He was just here to relax, to have a nice, quiet break, before continuing his trek.

A couple of the young men were still laughing, and one of them jostled the other the man who'd already eaten two sandwiches and drunk two beers. The fellow reached out, snatching one of his friend's sandwiches and taking a big bite.

The offended fellow yelped and pushed the hand away. The beefy boy who had stolen the bite was laughing now.

"Get your own," said the other.

The food thief shrugged and replied, "Maybe I will." He raised his hand, extending it in the direction of the waitress to call her over.

The waitress returned, water and bread on her tray. She paused at the other table and said, "Yes?"

"Another beer, and another order of the same," the man said, burping loudly.

The waitress hesitated, lowering her voice, "You know you have to pay for all of that, right? I remember you from last month. I didn't say anything because I didn't want to cause trouble. But my boss will fire me if you guys leave without paying again."

The young man shrugged, snickering and waving away her protests. The girl sighed, returning to the fridge to grab another beer and then placing it on the young man's table. No sooner had it clinked against the marble than he lifted it, twisted the cap, and began to chug.

Another sign.

The man sat straighter in his own booth, his eyes fixed on the unrepentant waif.

He could've gone into any sandwich shop. He could have stopped anywhere. He could've tired at any point. But he had stopped here and entered this shop.

What were the odds?

The good Lord was giving him a sign; he knew it. He couldn't stop. No matter how much he wanted to, he knew what he had to do. He couldn't disobey God himself.

He crossed himself, murmuring a soft prayer beneath his breath. The young man was a glutton. A thief. A drunkard. He had to answer for his sins. Yes. It would be the path forward. The next step, the proper response to the call of God.

He gritted his teeth, slowly reaching up to his head and adjusting his bangs once more. The woman brought over the water and the bread. He thanked her politely, not making eye contact. She said something, but he didn't reply. Conversation would lead to temptation. Besides, he had something of his own to focus on now. The glutton would have to respond for his actions. Soon. Very soon.

The waitress moved away again, and as she did, the man took a salt packet from next to the napkin holder.

He had behaved well today and he was going to respond in obedience. Perhaps, for tonight, he wouldn't have to punish himself so greatly. There were different levels to penance. Irritation was for a good day. Pain for a bad one. Today had been good.

He tore the salt packet, and then, when no one was looking, he pulled the waistband of his pants and poured the salt into his underwear. He did it again, and then again. One of the men at the table across from him shot him a confused look as his hand returned with the salt packet toward the surface of the table. But the man ignored them. He shifted a bit, uncomfortable all of a sudden, feeling the grains against his skin. He winced, but nodded to himself.

This was the appropriate response.

He took a bite of his bread. And a sip from his glass of water. He watched the glutton, watched the way he laughed and drank and was loud and swallowed, scarfing down another sandwich.

They would talk very soon.

CHAPTER FOURTEEN

Agent Pascal broke every speed limit there was, and this time even John's knuckles were white against the seat. Adele could feel her stomach twist as they sped down the road, moving through traffic.

"How much further?" Adele said through gritted teeth.

Pascal replied cheerfully, "Oh, don't worry, we made good time. I shaved off seven minutes."

"Really?" Adele said, as they swept around the side of a large truck and moved behind a sedan before merging sharply into the right lane and passing on the left side. "It felt longer," she gasped.

Her heart hammered, but her eyes fixed through the windshield. Every time they passed a truck, she glanced at the stenciled letters on the side. Nothing yet. But they were on the right route. The journey to Bilbao. He wouldn't reach his destination for another twenty minutes. And they were already catching up.

"He should be here soon," said Pascal. "It might make sense for us to just wait for him at the next destination."

Adele hesitated, but then nodded. "Where's that?"

"According to his itinerary he has to pull off at a truck stop three miles down the road. He's due to arrive in the next five minutes."

Adele perked up; John, who was still gripping the door like he wanted to rip it off, also looked over attentively. Agent Pascal continued to imitate a needle through fabric, sewing her way through traffic and further down the highway.

Northern Spain passed in a blur, with the occasional vehicle leaning on its horn. These blaring sounds didn't last long, though, when the irritated drivers realized a police cruiser was moving between them. The siren was off for now, along with the lights. They couldn't alert the driver—*not yet.*

Soon, though, they might need more backup.

Would Mr. Lazar be violent? Would he come with them quietly? He had motive, having proven to be violent with hitchhikers in the past. He also had visited the commune on his route for months now.

"There," John said, suddenly, "I can't read the word, but is that the rest stop?"

Pascal glanced up at the sign they whipped under and said, "I missed it. I think so." A few moments later, "Ah, yes. See there."

"How much further?" Adele said.

"Two miles," Pascal replied, cheerful as ever. She raced through traffic, and, ahead, Adele also spotted the outline of trucks now, lining a refueling station and rest stop.

"The itinerary says he has to stop here? For how long?" Adele said, wondering if perhaps they might have already missed him.

"He'll be here for half an hour," said Pascal. "Then continue on to Bilbao. We have ample time. He isn't due to arrive for another few minutes."

Adele felt her excitement mounting. She glanced over her shoulder, looking at other trucks as the police cruiser began to slow, approaching the exit to the rest stop.

"Hang on," John said, suddenly.

Adele frowned, and she followed the tall agent's pointed finger. He was indicating something on the other side of the rest stop.

A truck that looked like it had only recently arrived, instead of pulling in with the other trucks, was circling immediately toward the exit.

"Hang on, what does it say on the side of that panel?" Adele said rapidly.

All of them were quiet for a moment, and Pascal even slowed. For a moment, as they pulled forward, Adele waited with bated breath. And then she spotted the stenciling of a triangle on the side, and a single word: *Passo.*

She cursed. "That's it. That's his truck!"

John began to pump his fist, laughing in excitement. But the joviality died when the Frenchman realized the Passo truck wasn't pulling into the rest stop, but rather continued its path circling out, back toward the highway.

"Hang on," John muttered, "why isn't it stopping?"

Pascal, hesitant, slowed near the exit, but not quite taking it just yet. They had another quarter mile of road before she would have to commit completely.

"He should be," she said, firmly. "He's required to pull over for half an hour. He's already too early."

John growled. "Unless one of his buddies at the company tipped him we were looking for him," he retorted. "You said your contact spoke with them directly."

Agent Pascal's normally cheerful expression flickered into something like a frown. She shook her head. "You think that's

70

possible?"

John pointed in answer as the large truck pulled out of the exit, onto the highway again and began to pick up speed.

"More than possible," John snapped. "He's running. Go, go!"

Pascal didn't need a second invitation. She floored the pedal, once more jetting through the cars, tires squealing as she took them back out into the middle road.

As they maneuvered, Pascal reached down, switching on the sirens and lights. The front of the car and the windshield suddenly illuminated with strobes of red and blue.

Adele's heart was pounding so wildly now she thought it might cave in her chest.

They picked up the pace, faster and faster, rapidly speeding across the asphalt. Another car leaned on its horn, but then pulled over sharply.

Other cars were moving out of the way, allowing them to cut through the traffic like a hot knife through butter.

The truck ahead of them, though, was only picking up speed.

Pascal leaned on her horn, the sirens wailing, but the truck didn't seem to care. It continued speeding, racing as fast as it could away from them. And yet, the smaller police cruiser was gaining. Now, the trucker reached an exit. To continue on to Bilbao, he ought to have gone straight. Instead, though, he veered sharply, and for a horrible moment, Adele thought he might have tipped his cab.

Thankfully, especially for the cars around him, the truck slammed back to the ground and sped up this exit now, moving radically through traffic.

"We need to stop him," Pascal said, sharply, "he's endangering others."

No sooner had she said this than she also veered sharply, the tires squealing, Adele's body was thrown to the side, her shoulder bouncing off the door. John let out a little yelp.

They sped up the exit, moving through the trail the truck had already carved. Other vehicles were pulling off to the shoulder; one slammed into a concrete barrier, smashing its headlights.

The truck was moving so wildly, it clipped into the side of a minivan, crumpling one of the doors and sending the vehicle spinning out onto the shoulder. As they past, John gritted his teeth. "Get closer. Get that guy to stop."

Pascal was already on her radio, barking instructions to paramedics and backup. After a few moments, a voice replied, emanating from the speaker in the car.

Pascal said, "We have his radio frequency. Want me to contact him?"

"The trucker?" John said, suddenly. "You can do that? Yes. Yes, do that right now."

Pascal yammered something off in Spanish, and a reply returned. The response was short, curt. Pascal quickly entered something on the radio. A few moments passed, and then there was a static voice on the other side.

The fellow on the other end replied in French. Passo National was based out of Adele's country, though it delivered through Spain.

"Pull over," Adele said, shouting at the radio receiver. "Stop running and pull over, now!"

There was a long pause. Then a slurred voice, "Leave me alone. I didn't do anything!"

The truck was still picking up speed, now nearing a hundred mph. If he hit anything, the enormous weight of his vehicle would crush another car like a tin can.

"You're hurting people," Adele snapped. "Pull over now."

"Get off my tail," the voice retorted, still full of static. "Go away."

Adele cursed and Agent Pascal pulled into the right lane, trying to come alongside the truck.

Now, both vehicles were going faster. Both were racing breakneck down the evening highway. Other cars were quickly pulling out of the way, or, judging by some of the vehicles further ahead, responding to the sirens and moving into one of the slower lanes of traffic. The truck was still moving side to side, threatening to tip.

"John," Adele said. "He's gonna hit someone."

Even as she said it, a smaller vehicle, inattentive or unaware, put on its blinkers, trying to merge into the fast lane to reach an exit. The truck didn't stop. It slammed into the back of the smaller car, sending it spinning.

Adele cursed as glass scattered across the road.

Thankfully, the smaller car had been going speedily as well. Its tires squeaked, leaving rubber against the asphalt, but the driver kept control long enough to slow down and pull sharply to the side of the road. The driver leaned on his horn. But the truck didn't slow.

John cursed; he'd seen enough. He rolled down his window, his hand darting to his holster. His weapon appeared in his fist as if it were an extension of himself. John Renee was a crack shot. He was more experienced with his weapon than Adele was. And now, as Pascal drove alongside the truck, keeping pace, John poked his head out the window, his large arm extended past the windshield of the police cruiser, his skin also strobing with red and blue as the flashing lights caught his silhouette. He aimed, his face contorted into an expression of extreme concentration. Adele glimpsed his jaw tighten from where she sat in the back, his hair whipping around him. He aimed.

The truck driver seemed to realize what was happening and began to suddenly swerve.

John fired twice.

The back tire exploded.

The loud whirring of wheels suddenly was replaced by a dull *thumping* sound. The truck began to slow, still rocking. The trailer tipped back and forth precariously as one wheel lifted and then hit the road.

Pascal slowed, careful to avoid the sliding back of the giant truck.

The vehicle was now on its last legs. John aimed again, fired twice more. The front tire exploded. And this time, the truck began to veer into the middle lane. Pascal cursed, pulling to the side, and then muttered beneath her breath, "I apologize for the foul language."

Adele didn't have time to make much of this. She was shouting herself. "Cut him off! Cut him off before he hits anyone!"

Pascal, to her credit, didn't balk at the instruction. Showing more than a small amount of courage, she guided their own, far smaller vehicle toward the front of the truck. The larger truck was slowing now, missing two wheels, the tread of the rubber of one left behind them now.

A loud scraping sound accompanying sparks shot out from the wheel wells.

"Pull over!" Adele screamed into the radio.

"*Merde!*" the voice snapped back.

As Pascal nosed in front of the truck, keeping her distance, but making her intentions clear, the vehicle finally began to slow.

A few moments passed and then it came to a steaming, smoking, scraping halt in the center of the highway. A few cars behind them finally caught up, leaning on their horns as they veered around the cars. The ground was streaked with black marks from the truck's remaining two wheels. John was already flinging open the door and racing out. "Hands up!" Renee was shouting, his voice booming. "Put your hands where I can see them now!" he screamed.

Adele watched, also pushing open her door, moving a bit slower, careful, trying to keep track of every moving part. Then, two hands jutted out of the window of the front seat of the truck. She felt her heart hammer, her voice squeaking as she said, "Thank God."

Pascal was drumming her fingers against the steering wheel, speaking back to the radio, saying things like, "Just stay calm. It's going to be okay. Please remain calm."

John rounded the front of the truck, his face red, his hair out of place. He pointed at the trucker in the cabin. "Get out here," John bellowed. "Get out now!"

Adele reached John's side, her own weapon in hand, aimed toward the ground.

Trembling fingertips reached for the external handle of the door, and there was an ominous *click*. For a moment, the sound hung in the air like the faint tap of a judge's gavel, bringing proceedings to a halt. Then the door swung open slowly, with an air of ultimate reluctance.

A bald man with a beer gut and mean eyes glared down at them from the cabin. Gabino Lazar. The same face as the mug shot she'd been shown.

"Down, *now*," snapped Adele.

The man cursed, spitting off to the side, but then, glaring at each of them in turn, he slipped out of the cabin, and, careful not to make any sudden movements, he lowered to the asphalt. Adele noticed his hands were twitching, his face slicked with sweat, his eyes bloodshot.

A second later, John steamed forward, slamming an elbow into the man and sending him ricocheting off the side of the truck. He twisted the man's arm behind his back, ignoring the protestations of the trucker.

"I didn't do anything!" he was yelling. "You had no right. I didn't do anything!"

Adele glanced back at the many cars on the side of the road, some visibly damaged. She scowled and said, "Well you did now. You're coming with us, Mr. Lazar."

"Why?" he said, desperately, his voice nearing a moan. "What did I do? What is this about?"

"Murder, Mr. Lazar," Adele said testily, finding some of her adrenaline fading now that they'd come to a standstill. "We want to speak with you about murder. Stop struggling—you're not going anywhere."

His face went pale, and he made a burping sound. "I—dear God. I think I'm going to be sick. His eyelids fluttered. "I need help—medics. Please. Take me to a doctor."

A thin bead of sweat dappled the man's forehead, and he continued to gasp, face against the metal of the truck.

CHAPTER FIFTEEN

A strange thing how dots connected. The painter smiled, enjoying the sunny weather San Francisco offered all comers. The city was treating him quite well. Perhaps one day he'd even consider moving here. Then again, given what he had planned, that might not be the best option.

He curled the small paper straw around his finger like a ring, watching as it unwound again, before curling it once more.

He whistled beneath his breath, sitting in the cafe across the street from his target.

Every masterpiece required patience. The true greats, the ones who had perfected their craft, those were the ones who could be the most patient.

A couple of cars passed in the other direction, making almost no noise. Electric vehicles. Almost everywhere. Not the sort of thing he'd seen too often in France.

He waited a moment longer, eyes on the apartment. It had once been *her* apartment. He smiled at the thought. He couldn't wait until she found out that he knew. But then again, everything came in its proper time.

He curled the straw again, watching it unwind. He held up a hand as a waiter came by, carrying a menu. The waiter hesitated and began to say, "Sir, if you're not going to order, I'm afraid you can't—"

The painter looked at him, staring with one dull eye. He didn't blink, and he didn't say anything. He didn't try to rearrange his features or look intimidating in any way. But he'd long ago learned that people saw something when he met their gaze. He'd looked in the mirror before, as a self-study. He never could quite understand what they were reacting to. He did have odd features, after a fashion. But what great artist didn't? Van Gogh had cut off his own ear.

And yet, the effect was universal. The waiter stared at him for a moment, swallowed, and then babbled an apology, before quickly retreating.

The painter lazily looked away again, eyes on the apartment doors.

He checked his watch. Soon. It would have to be soon.

And then the door buzzed. A figure emerged. A man with curly

75

brown hair. A straight nose, pale features, and glasses. He was quite handsome, in a desk job kind of way.

His case study began to move down the sidewalk, chatting idly on a telephone via a Bluetooth speaker.

Inattentive. This would be easier than he thought.

The painter got slowly to his feet, careful not to make any sound. The man with the curly hair crossed to the side of the street with the cafe, moving down the sidewalk, still yammering away.

He passed within a few feet of the painter. He didn't even look up. He didn't see a thing.

The painter whistled a bit more, allowing the straw to uncurl around his finger and then tossing it on the table. He began to move after the man with the curly hair. He wondered what Adele would think when this was all done. Would she blame herself?

He certainly hoped not. He didn't like sharing credit.

This was his doing. Adele was simply the blessed one. Not every artist had a muse. When he had found his, he could feel the difference in his artwork. Everyone could feel it.

He smiled, picking up the pace, following after the man and maneuvering down the sidewalk. He kept his distance. Now he was just gathering information. Biding his time. Enjoying himself. He watched the way the man's arms moved against the thin fabric of his long shirt. He tracked the musculature of his legs. The way his feet pointed out just a bit too far. The man's hands kept twitching and moving and curling. He had a nervous tic where he reached up and tugged at one ear.

All of these little things had to be noticed for a true artist. Beauty was in the details.

Still whistling softly beneath his breath, limping faintly, the painter followed after his new friend, moving along the sidewalk, completely unnoticed, unobserved, and ignored.

The calm before the storm.

And this time, it would be a hurricane.

***

Adele could feel her frustration mounting as she watched the paramedics examine their suspect in the back of the ambulance. Evening had turned to night, and the flash of headlights passing them on the highway acted like errant spotlights illuminating the vehicles pulled to the side of the road.

A portion of the rest stop had been cleared, allowing for the police vehicles and the ambulance to occupy space. Now, as Adele watched the paramedics work, one of the men looked over at her, flashed a thumbs-up and a quick nod. He raised five fingers and tapped his wrist, before turning and rounding the front of his vehicle. A second later, the other paramedic followed. They reached in the front seat, pulling out a clipboard, and began to quickly move through a checklist.

Five minutes. That's how long the paramedics had given them to speak with the man before they had to take him to a hospital.

Adele was beginning to wonder if they were going out of their way to protect innocents or criminals more. Still, five minutes was more than nothing. John was currently speaking with another CNI agent, explaining why he had discharged his weapon on Spanish soil. Adele didn't know how much red tape would be involved. Already, they had been forced to notify Agent Paige. It wasn't after eight yet either. Which meant her children weren't in bed. Things were just getting worse.

Adele approached the back of the ambulance where the man was cuffed to a cot. He was sitting up, dazedly looking out at the police cars gathered at the corner of the rest stop. His eyes were still bloodshot, and he couldn't seem to quite hold himself upright, swaying even where he sat.

"Mr. Lazar," said Adele, carefully, "this has been a rough night."

The man looked at her and for a moment he blinked, as if trying to get her in focus. "Rough," he repeated, nodding once.

"Sir, why did you run?"

The man hesitated, and then, slurring his words as he spoke, he said, "Is this true? You think I killed someone?"

Adele blinked, glancing toward where the paramedics were still checking their boxes. "Let me ask the questions, please."

The man just rattled his handcuffs against the side of the cart. "I didn't kill anyone," he said, still slurring. "I thought, I thought you were here about something else."

"Sir, I spoke to the paramedics before they checked you out. They seem to think you're on some sort of methamphetamine."

"Hang on," he protested, "hang on, I know, look, I know, it technically breaks my parole. But hear me out. Hear me out. Hear me out," he repeated the third time as if he were stuck on the phrase.

"I'm listening," she said.

"Look, I just take a little something to help me focus and stay awake."

Adele frowned. "We checked your records. When you were imprisoned you had to be put in detox. You had a meth issue then too. Long before you were a trucker."

He sighed, shaking his head morosely. "I didn't kill anyone," he said, muttering beneath his breath.

Adele nodded. She could feel a flicker of doubt. The violation of his parole might have been enough for him to flee the police. What she had initially taken for a sign of guilt might have been indicating some other portion of a guilty conscience with nothing to do with her murders. Still, even as she felt her energies receding like a deflating balloon, she knew she had to at least be certain. "Sir, I need to know where you were yesterday."

"Yesterday?"

"Yes."

"Wasn't killing anyone. That's for sure."

"Sir. You're in a lot of trouble. Maybe you can forget the attitude and just tell me what I want to know."

The man snorted. But at a look in her eyes, he sobered a bit, still shaking his head and twitching, his words still slurred as he said, "On my route, well, mostly. All right, don't tell my boss."

"Sir, you're in violation of your parole. Your boss is the least of your worries right now."

He uttered a series of choice curse words, shaking his head in frustration. After a moment, though, he calmed enough to say, "Can't you cut me a little slack? Like I said, I was trying my best."

"I'll put in a good word if you answer my questions. Where were you yesterday?"

"I wasn't driving," he said, still slurring. "I should've been. It was my route. I admit it." He slammed her fist against his chest, his handcuff rattling in its full extension. "But," he said, emphatically, "I did not. Bardem ran it for me. He's a good guy. I like him."

Adele stared. "Bardem?"

He nodded. "My friend. He once served time too. He gets it."

"This Mr. Bardem covered your route for you yesterday?"

"Yes. I was stuck."

"I don't understand."

"Stuck in the city. I was drunk. And a little high. But keep that between us." He spoke this part conspiratorially, holding a finger to his lips as if to shush her.

"You were high, so your friend took your route for you. And you were staying in which city?"

"Santander. One of my favorite places is there. I stay there all the time. Say, if you're looking for an alibi, Bardem can tell you. Everyone saw me at the hotel."

Adele could feel the sinking sensation had now reached the bottom of her stomach. She felt like she wanted to puke. "So you're telling me you weren't anywhere near Santo Domingo de Silos?"

"No. Like I said, I should've been. But I didn't complete my route. I got my truck again today and started heading to Bilbao."

Adele could feel her frustration mounting. The odd scheduling might have accounted for why he had showed up at the rest stop before they had. He had never been near the old abbey. Never been near where Rosa had been killed.

"This friend of yours, the one who you say ran your truck, I'm going to need his phone number."

"Hang on, wait. He didn't do anything wrong. I vouch for him. He's a good guy."

"I believe you. I just need him to confirm your story. And the name of the hotel, please."

"You're not going to tell my boss, are you?"

"Sir, for the sake of your *friend's* job, I'll keep this between us. You have my word. But I need you to tell me everything so I can verify your story. I'm not here about your drug problem; that's between you and the parole board. I'm looking for a killer. And I need you to be honest so I can do my job."

The man stared blearily at the ground for a moment, letting out a soft little sigh. He looked like a child who had been reprimanded—so sad, alone, chained in the back of an ambulance. It seemed hard to believe this was the same guy tearing through traffic and sending cars careening off the side of the road. She wondered what those people would've thought of Mr. Lazar. For her part, she just felt sad. And also disappointed. She would have to double-check his story. Call the hotel, call Mr. Bardem, but in the end, she had a sinking suspicion the alibi would check out. A man in this state, addicted as he was, would not be in any sort of condition to chase down a healthy young woman and cut her throat.

By his testimony, he hadn't even been in the province.

She cursed beneath her breath, pulling out her phone as, reluctantly, Mr. Lazar rattled off the phone number for his alibi.

CHAPTER SIXTEEN

He strolled through the street. He didn't like strolling. He preferred a brisk pace or jog. But the glutton was still with his friends. They were tossing rocks at some of the trees as they passed, laughing as they did. None of them were in a car. Strange. Most folks used vehicles. But they were on the French Way, after all. Certainly the glutton was beyond absolution, wasn't he?

The father continued to stroll beneath the night, as the moon watched their progress witnessing the way he stalked in their footsteps. His undergarments itched. He could feel the hot grains of salt and winced in discomfort, but kept his hands at his side, walking straight, stiff-backed.

"Sinner!" the voice from his youth shouted. *"Sinner!"* The memory brought to mind the thwack of the rod against his back.

He had been trained from a young age. Destined for greatness. He didn't like what he had to do. But God had brought him to the glutton. And so he would have to see it through.

He watched as the three men pulled alongside the small house with a plaque out front that read *Pilgrim's Hostel.*

He waited as the young men walked up the steps, laughing to each other and then knocking on the front door. A second passed and it opened, sending white light out into the darkness, as the men were ushered into the two-story home turned hostel.

He waited, standing by the fence for a moment. Once the quiet had returned, confident he wouldn't have to interact with too many people and face temptation, he moved into the garden, up the pathway, up the steps. He paused in front of the door, pulled out his cotton handkerchief, placing it against the doorframe, and then knocked against the cotton. He stepped back, waiting, returning his handkerchief to his pocket. The door swung open.

An older woman with laugh lines and an easy smile was standing in the door, gesturing for him to enter.

"Come in, come in," she said, cheerfully. "You're welcome. We still have rooms. How long is your stay going to be?"

He stared at her. A very wide smile that. Was she trying to tempt him? He could sense it. He could feel it on her. Promiscuity was loathed by the Lord. And there she was, staring at him, offering her body as if it wasn't worth anything. Disgusting.

But he had to focus. He could only follow one command at a time.

"One room," he said, frowning.

"Well, we do have a couple, or a room with one of those boys you saw coming."

"Which one?"

She wrinkled her nose, stepping back behind a small desk that approximated a hotel room's lobby. It was much smaller and seemed handcrafted in the entry room of the house. "Which one? I don't know. But it's cheaper."

"Frugality is next to wisdom," he said.

She gave him a long look, her smile diminishing a bit. Good. She'd seen the error of her ways. She had repented. But the glutton wasn't nearly so contrite.

"I'll take the shared room," he said. "Communal living is of the Lord."

Now she was frowning. This bordered on disrespect. But he had to focus on one command at a time.

"Keys, please," he said. He pulled out his wallet, withdrawing a couple of bills.

"All right, and what name should I write down for the room?"

"Ricardo Mora," he said, paused, but then said, "I—no... No, that's a lie. I'm sorry. I apologize. That's not my real name. But I am not going to lie to you again. I'm not going to give you my name."

She now just stared at him. After a moment, she shrugged, muttering beneath her breath something that sounded like, "All sorts of crazies tonight..."

But his money was good enough for her, and she took it, pointing toward the stairwell. "Your roommate is going to be up soon. His friends wanted to use the facilities first. The bathroom is downstairs. Please don't use the one upstairs—that's private. In addition, if you would like a breakfast tomorrow morning, that's extra. We do not serve lunch or dinner. Have a great stay. Thank you."

He nodded to show he had heard, but didn't reply. No sense in engaging with a newly repentant sinner. He might entice her back into her old lascivious ways.

He turned toward the stairs, glancing over his shoulder, through the open door, down the street toward where he had locked his bike.

One step at a time. One command at a time. He took the stairs, moving up toward the second floor and the indicated room.

***

Matthew entered his new room, feeling a slight buzz from the three beers he had downed back at that sandwich shop. He normally didn't like cheap beer, but the waitress was cute. He liked talking with her. Now, he had gotten the short end of the stick. His friends would be sharing a room and he had to bunk up with some stranger.

He grumbled to himself a bit as he pushed open the door completely and stepped into the bedroom on the second floor.

His roommate was already there. The man sat on a bunk, facing the window, his head bowed, his hands clasped as if in prayer

Matthew hesitated for a moment, sighing to himself, but then stepped into the room, hefting his backpack and dropping it on the second bed on the other side of the room.

"Please close the door," said the older man.

Matthew sighed, returning to the door and closing it with a quiet *click*.

"Hi, I'm Matthew," he said, waving his hand vaguely.

The older man looked over and smiled. "Hello, Matthew. You have a good name."

"Er, okay then. Thanks. What's yours?"

Instead of answering, the man said, "Why are you here, Matthew?"

"You mean like in the room? Probably to get some sleep."

"No, I mean traveling here, staying in a hostel."

"Oh. Well. It's kind of funny actually," he said, hesitantly, scratching at his chin. Matthew felt uncomfortable all of a sudden. His two other friends had agreed to come here with him, though they wouldn't be walking the pilgrimage alongside him. Neither of them came from religious families. None of them had his traditions. Not that he considered himself particularly religious at all. But if he ever told his dad no, that would be the end of free rent.

"I'm walking the St. James Way," he said with a shrug. "It's a little bit like a family tradition."

The man on the bed perked up, nodding. He shifted and a few grains of what looked like sand fell on the ground beneath his leg.

Matthew wrinkled his nose. Had the man just come from a beach somewhere?

"Your family believes in the way?"

"Honestly," Matthew said, airily, waving a hand and letting out a long burp, "I just do it for the free rent at my dad's place. If I don't do it, he'd probably kick me out."

The man on the bed just nodded politely, his hands folded in his lap.

"What are *you* doing here?" Matthew wasn't really in the mood for conversation, but the man had started it, and if they were going to be sleeping in the same room, he figured at least he could establish some sort of rapport and not have to be worried about getting stabbed in his sleep.

"Now, Matthew," the man said, deftly ignoring the question again, "you expect to travel the French Way in the footsteps of St. James and arrived at the shrine? You are looking for absolution?"

"I mean, yeah. I guess. So you know about it?"

"See, Matthew, the thing about absolution, which is quite hard, is you can extend past it. Think of a rubber band." The man shifted, his boots scraping against some of the sand on the ground. He pulled something out of his pocket, holding it up. A seashell. A large, thick, slick seashell.

"What is that?"

Another question ignored. The old man twisted the seashell around and around, smiling as he did. "Absolution is a gift."

Matthew was beginning to grow uncomfortable. He hadn't signed up for a lecture from a stranger. "All right, guy. Whatever you say."

"Listen to me, Matthew," the man said, his voice hoarse. "I'm tempted to lose my temper. But that would be impatient. A sin. You understand what sin is?"

Matthew rubbed at the bridge of his nose. He hadn't want to pay extra, but to get away from this weirdo, he wouldn't mind. He needed to sleep anyway. This was gonna be the last fun day he had in a while with his buddies.

"Whatever," he said as a parting shot, turning toward the door, snatching his backpack, and heading to grab the handle.

The man was quick, though, bounding out of the bed and coming to a halt in front of the door, holding his strange seashell.

"Hey, get out of my way."

"Matthew, please listen to me, you have to understand why. It isn't my intention to cause unnecessary pain. Please. Penance, absolution, such things are important."

"Man, I don't know any of this stuff. Plenary indulgence, St. James, whatever. It's all crap. I'm just doing it. All right, now move. Move or I'll make you. I mean it!"

The man paused, standing upright. He had very neatly parted hair, like a choir boy. He stood straight-backed with perfect posture.

83

At these last words, though, his eyes narrowed. "I'm afraid I'm going to have to punish you."

At this, Matthew felt an odd combination of cringe and terror. A chill trickled down his spine. "Get out of my way. I mean it, man!"

"Yes, it's the way. I don't like what I have to do to you. But the Lord told me. I'm sorry, Matthew."

He took a step back now, hesitant, slowly lifting his backpack like a shield.

But then the strange man bolted forward, fast. Matthew tried to jerk away, but the man lunged, shoving him against the bed. Matthew kicked, trying to scream, but fingers grabbed over his lips, and the sound was cut off. The odd seashell came whipping forward. It jammed into his neck hard, slicing.

Matthew yelled now, but his voice was cut off a second later. His eyes widened in panic, kicking, screaming, desperately trying to get free. But most of the sounds were muffled by the hand over his mouth. His violent motions weren't enough to dislodge his strong roommate. More pain on his neck. Two eyes above him, unblinking, staring. A single word whispered, "Repent."

And then the pain became so intense, his eyes rolled back in panic and terror; then he fainted.

CHAPTER SEVENTEEN

The chill air of night, replacing the swaddling warmth of daylight, settled in Adele's bones. She stared after the retreating ambulance, watching as the paramedics, escorted by two police cars, took Mr. Lazar to the hospital. Adele's hands dangled at her sides, her phone gripped between clenched fingers, her eyes on the flashing lights of the highway.

Mr. Bardem, Mr. Lazar's coworker, had confirmed the man's alibi. She'd already requested a confirmation of the phone number's identity and was waiting—tentatively—for Agent Pascal to get back to her. But she wasn't hopeful.

Mr. Lazar had been erratic, dangerous, but hardly subtle. Not the sort of man to stalk someone until they were alone and kill them in the dark, in privacy.

No… Mr. Lazar's alibi had checked out. Holding on to hope that it would all crumble wouldn't be the best use of her time.

What then?

Adele wrinkled her nose, still staring in the direction of the whining ambulance, watching as cars parted before it.

"Bad news," a gruff voice muttered behind her.

Adele looked over at the side of the concrete barrier on the edge of the highway. John was stalking toward her, scowling and shaking his head. He jerked a thumb in the direction of their parked cruiser where Agent Pascal was still on the phone. "No go. The alibi checks out. Mr. Bardem works for the same company. Admits to taking over his friend's route as a favor."

Adele sighed. "Same news from the hotel," she said, slowly slipping her phone back into her pocket. "They had a man matching Mr. Lazar's description check in and stay the night."

"More than two hours from where Ms. Alvarez was killed that same day."

Adele and John both sighed at the same time. Adele felt sore all of a sudden, wincing and massaging her neck. It was all so exhausting.

What next? What new lead could they uncover?

Maybe the victims weren't connected after all—maybe the murderer was just arbitrarily executing anyone he found. In some ways, it was harder to catch a maniac—they were less predictable in the mayhem they caused.

As these morbid thoughts cycled through her mind, she heard a soft ringtone and glanced over as John's hand darted to his pocket. He hesitated, almost as if he were going to let the call go to voicemail.

And now this… John acting strange again.

Perhaps he didn't deserve it, but Adele could feel her temper rising, could feel her frustration mounting. She fixated her gaze on John and said, through gritted teeth, "Answer it."

John paused, hand still on his pocket. He began to speak, but she cut him off.

"I mean it. Answer it now, John. Who the hell keeps calling you? What are you hiding?"

John stared at her, but seemed to realize she was being serious and, with a sigh, he pulled out his device, lifting it and wiggling it in her direction. For a moment, as he glanced at the screen, he almost seemed relieved. Or was it just her imagination? She was so tired…

"Ha, see!" John said, as if he'd just scored some point. "It's just Agent Pascal."

Adele turned, peering past the concrete barrier toward where the tall, large-framed woman was holding her phone to her cheek and gesturing at them to come over to where she stood, talking with a Spanish police sergeant.

Adele hesitated at the frown on the normally cheerful woman's face.

John answered, paused, then said, "You sure?"

Pascal, in answer, over by the rest stop, just waved again, her arm small against the backdrop of the night, the reflection of passing headlights flashing across the paint of her borrowed cruiser.

"What is it?" Adele said petulantly. Both times now she'd called John out on the phone calls, she'd been wrong. She hated eating crow. But he was acting strange, wasn't he? Or was she just insane? She rubbed at the bags under her eyes, focusing on John once more and forcing a calmer tone. "What does she want?"

John was already moving, though, heading in the direction of their parked cruiser, navigating the concrete barrier on the side of the road and maneuvering past the officers stationed, blocking this section of the rest stop.

As Adele moved to keep up with her lanky partner, she heard John mutter, "Another body. They found it just south of here."

Adele's skin prickled and she stared from her partner over to where

Agent Pascal was still standing, frowning and speaking with the other officer.

"Same killer? We're sure?"

"Same rough cut… No autopsy report yet about calcium carbonate, but the same MO otherwise. Throat slit—no one saw anything."

"Where?" Adele said, her pulse racing.

"At a hostel an hour away. This time," he muttered, "I'm driving."

***

Pascal drove them to the hostel nearly an hour away, despite John's best efforts to take the driver's seat. Now, Adele hopped out of the back seat as they slid smoothly into the driveway of a quaint two-story home with a laminated placard out front declaring vacancy in the communal living space.

John slammed the car door as he hurried to catch up, muttering to himself about carsickness.

Adele shouldered through the house, entrance which was already open. She heard voices from within and, stepping past a man in a police uniform, her gaze settled on a woman standing behind the desk, her eyes etched with laugh lines. Now, though, the woman had a hand to her mouth, her face displaying evidence of recent tears. She seemed to have calmed herself, though, and was now speaking to the police officer.

The officer looked over at Adele and John as they moved in. Adele flashed her ID and said, "Hello, English? French?"

The woman behind the counter raised a hand which clutched used tissue. She pressed the tissue back to an eye, lowering it again. In broken English, she said, "No more vacancy. Sorry."

"No, no," Adele said, raising her ID again. "DGSI. We're law enforcement."

Agent Pascal was now moving up behind them, content to stand outside the open door and watch the proceedings from the porch. The officer who was already there leaned in, muttering to the woman, his eyes brightening in recognition. Pascal returned the murmur and the officer's eyebrows shot up, the look he cast toward John and Adele now no longer as suspicious.

"I'm sorry," Adele said, hurriedly, taking this as a sort of permission to cut in on the interview, "but you're the owner of this place?"

The woman behind the counter hesitated, as if translating the words

87

in her mind one at a time, but then she nodded quickly. "*Sí*, yes. I am owner."

"And the victim is where?"

She pointed up and broke into a round of sobs, clutching the tissue against her face and ducking her head.

"I'm sorry," Adele said gently. "I don't mean to upset you. Who found the body?"

The woman's face paled; she swallowed and murmured, "I find this. I find this."

"Again, I'm very sorry. When you found it... was there anything that stood out? Anything you noticed off about the room? Anything at all you can tell me?" Of course, she would observe the room herself soon enough. But she knew well how important first impressions were when arriving at a scene. The kind-eyed woman owned the place and would be in the perfect position to spot anything awry.

Now, though, the woman was just shaking her head, sobbing. "Dead," she said. "Murder."

"I know. I know," Adele said, still gently. "I'm very sorry." She could feel the others in the room all watching her, but pressed on. "Are there any other guests here?"

The woman nodded, holding up three fingers, but then pointing out the door and down the street. She said something, paused, and tried again.

"I—I'm sorry, what?" Adele asked.

Pascal called from the doorway, "She says the police have them at the cafe down the street, waiting for the crime scene to be cleared."

"I see," said Adele. She looked back at the owner of the hostel. "Anyone else?"

The owner paused, and then, carefully, as if picking her words from a menu, she said, "Man room in with boy."

"There was another person in the room?"

She nodded. "Yes. Room in the same."

"This man, is he at the cafe?"

Here, though, the woman's eyes widened and she shook her head. She looked past Adele, craning her neck to spot where Pascal stood, and began speaking rapidly in her own language. After a few moments, Pascal nodded and the woman ducked her head again, sobbing once more.

Adele looked at the CNI agent. "What did she say?"

Pascal shot a sympathetic glance at the woman, but then said, quietly, "She says that the victim had just ordered his room. He gave his name as Ricardo Mora, but then said he was lying about the name. He checked in only a few hours before she found the body. She went upstairs because the young man had left a wet towel on the floor in the shower and wanted him to take care of it. But when she entered the room…" Pascal rolled a finger as if to say *et cetera*.

"I see," said Adele. "What did she mean about the man lying about his name?"

Pascal translated the question, waited, and, after a few more stops and starts as the landlord gathered herself, she eventually turned back to Adele. "She says the man was another tenant who stayed in the same room. He refused to give his name. He also only just arrived. After the victim."

"How long after?" Adele said sharply.

This time, the hostel owner replied, "Ten minute. Only ten minute. Very nearly. Very nearly."

"I see," said Adele, her pulse accelerating. "This man, do you think you could describe him to me?"

The woman paused as Pascal repeated the instruction, but then shrugged. "Nice," she said. "Look nice. Normal."

"What color hair, do you remember? Skin tone? Height?"

She puffed a breath, hesitant. She pointed at Adele. "Bit tall." Pointed at John. "Not as tall."

"Taller than me? By a bit?" Adele said.

The woman nodded.

"Anything else?"

"Hair brown? Maybe?"

"Brown hair in Spain, great," John muttered in French.

Adele shot him a warning look.

The woman shrugged again and said something Adele didn't understand which Pascal translated as, "She really couldn't say. She was so busy and didn't pay much attention. She says he acted a bit strangely."

"Strangely how?"

"She says he wasn't very talkative. He spoke like a school teacher. Sort of condescendingly."

"Great," Adele said. Brown-haired, average height, and condescending was hardly a description worthy of an APB. Still, she supposed it wasn't nothing. She nodded her gratitude toward the hostel owner and then, following John, moved toward the stairs leading to the second floor. The police officer behind them resumed his questioning as they took the stairs up to the top. Another officer was guarding the door on the left, but flashing her ID this time gained them entrance.

As the officer stepped aside and Adele pushed at the closed wooden door, a sudden smell met her nose. Tinny, coppery, like blood. And the sweaty, sweet smell of human BO.

As she pushed into the small room, she noted two beds on either side of the room framing the grisly spectacle across the floor. Blood was everywhere, first in streaks across the bed and then staining the wooden ground. A few droplets spattered the windowsill, which was open.

"Window," Adele murmured to John.

"Think that's how he got out?" John said.

"Looks like," Adele replied. Her eyes darted to the body on the ground.

A young man, a bit heftier than John and shorter. He had a nasty gash across his throat. Not so much one cut as multiple stitched together at odd, jagged angles.

Adele stared at the wound, stared at the young man's sightless eyes fixated on the wall and the radiator. Her own stomach churned and she felt an urge to yell. Another body. Another soul lost.

For a moment, she didn't speak, simply staring at the corpse, feeling the weight of the world descend on her shoulders and threaten to glue her to the ground. Her own breathing came in rapid puffs and her throat constricted as she stared at the young man. She noted a sandwich wrapper resting next to the man's hand, near the bed.

"What was his name?" she said, softly, her eyes still fixed on that horrible gash along his throat. Very similar to the first two victims. The same? Perhaps not... But odds were for it.

"Matthew Icardi," said a voice from the door.

Adele glanced back to see Agent Pascal standing there, her face rigid as she looked in any direction except the body. "He was only twenty," Pascal said, her voice wafer thin. "My son's age."

Adele didn't know how to reply to this. She simply sighed, shaking her head.

"He was a Spanish citizen," Pascal continued. "The police have checked his ID. From Barcelona. Apparently his friends said they were on a trip."

"His friends?" Adele said, dully.

"Yes—two of them at the cafe. They were in another room. Apparently they didn't even see the man who Matthew was with. According to the landlady the two of them were still taking a shower when our mystery killer arrived."

Adele glanced back at the corpse, shivering. "He was on a trip?"

"Apparently. They said he was going to meet his brother tomorrow."

"Has the brother been notified?"

Pascal sighed wearily, passing a hand across her face. "Yes. He is on his way."

CHAPTER EIGHTEEN

The cafe had been cleared now of the other tenants from the hostel, but Adele sat at a booth with John near the fridge, his arms crossed. Agent Pascal sat next to Adele, waiting patiently, her eyes darting toward the door.

"When did you say he was coming?" Adele murmured, her eyes half hooded as she watched the entrance to the now-empty cafe.

"Patrol officer picked him up a quarter hour ago," Pascal replied. "Should be here by now." She checked her watch, pulling her phone from her pocket. She didn't use it yet, preferring to rest it on the table and wait, still watching the door. Her fingers rested over her phone, not quite touching it, like a spider perched above a fly.

Adele could feel exhaustion weighing heavy now. She glanced at her own phone, noting the two text bubbles. Without even reading Agent Paige's most recent comment, Adele hastily typed, "Will keep you posted. Interviewing third victim's brother…" She then flipped her phone so she couldn't see the screen, growling in disgust.

"Everything all right?" Pascal asked, shooting a look toward Adele.

"Fine, fine. Just higher-ups causing headaches."

"Ah, yes. I understand. As it often is, heh?" She smiled, winking at Adele.

Despite herself, her own lips curled and Adele found herself growing even more fond of the broad-faced Spaniard. She didn't doubt that Serra Pascal's own supervisors were likely looking very closely over her shoulder as well. They had no real leads on the killer. The landlady's description had been tenuous at best. An approximate height, a common hair color, and a non-physical mannerism. They would have to put an APB out to the best of their ability, but Adele wasn't holding her breath. Not only that, the man in question hadn't even provided his real name to the owner of the hostel. She'd marked him down simply as Tenant Two in her ledger.

No name, no description, three victims—this man was on a rampage and Adele was falling further behind.

As these bleak thoughts cast her countenance in darkness, Adele's gaze darted toward the door, which was being pushed open by a woman in a blue uniform. She pressed a hand to the radio on her shoulder and then brusquely guided a young man through the door.

The fellow in question had a square face and a very thick, dark beard that didn't quite fit the youthfulness of his features.

He stepped tentatively into the cafe, rubbing one arm in a nervous gesture, wearing casual jeans and a ratty T-shirt.

"Hello," Adele said quickly, rising to her feet along with Agent Pascal. "Mr. Icardi?"

The man hesitated, swallowed, then nodded once.

"Do you know why you're here?" Adele said, gesturing quickly toward the empty chair across from where the agents sat.

After Pascal translated, the brother of the victim inhaled for a moment, then puffed a long breath. He nodded once.

Pascal translated, "He knows his brother is dead."

Adele watched the young man's expression as he approached. He looked shell-shocked more than anything, the pallor of his face not quite matching the sun-kissed hue of his arms. His hair was disheveled, like his shirt, and his hands kept tapping wildly against his thigh, drumming some complicated rhythm, which, every now and then, even included a snap of his fingers or a pat of his hand.

Adele pointed toward his fingers. "Are you a musician?"

"Drummer," Pascal translated.

The young man let out a long sigh as he settled in the empty seat, glancing blearily around the cafe as if he were certain he'd found himself trapped in a dream. After a moment, his drumming fingers found the table, then his leg again, quieter but still insistently tapping.

Adele ignored this, also sitting again and facing the young man. She arranged her features into as gentle an estimation as she could manage.

"I'm very, very sorry for your loss," she said softly.

The young man hesitated. Once Pascal spoke, he sighed and nodded. He paused, then said something else. Pascal replied, pointing through the cafe door in the direction of the small hostel down the street. She continued and the only phrase Adele managed to translate for herself was "...second floor..." and "...sorry..."

The young man, whom Pascal had called Giam Icardi, kept tapping his fingers. He muttered a few half-stuttered comments between the motions of his hands. At the end he just shrugged and sighed, staring at the table as if searching for something etched in the lacquer.

Pascal nodded her gratitude once he'd finished speaking and looked to Adele. "He says he was supposed to meet his brother not far from here. He says it is their family tradition to walk the Camino de Santiago pilgrimage."

"The what?" Adele said.

Pascal's eyebrows went up. "You don't know? The Way of St. James in English, I believe."

Adele hesitated, wracking her brain, but then shook her head. "No... No, I'm sorry, what is it?"

Pascal folded her arms, nodding. "I see. Well, the Camino de Santiago is a network of pilgrimages that cross through Spain—it takes eight to ten hours driving. But you're not supposed to drive. Eventually, the way leads to the shrine of the apostle Saint James the Great in Galicia at the cathedral of Santiago de Compestalo."

"I... All right. That's in Northern Spain?"

"Northwest, but yes."

"And he was walking the pilgrimage with his brother?"

Pascal said something in Spanish and Giam just nodded.

"I see," said Adele. "As a family tradition?"

Pascal nodded, her eyes carrying a soft sort of sadness. "Giam thought it would be fun to do with his brother. He never thought anything like this would happen. He says he doesn't know who would have hurt his brother. Who could have."

"Did Matthew have any enemies? Anyone who might have wanted to harm him?"

Pascal repeated the question, but Giam shook his head emphatically. After a second, though, he paused and, in a sheepish tone, muttered beneath his breath.

Pascal nodded, patting the table with her hand, not quite touching Giam but gesturing toward him. She said to Adele, "No one like that. Though, he did say Matthew could be a bit obnoxious at times. He wasn't a bad guy, but he could be nosy. Maybe that annoyed someone."

Adele sighed, gathering her thoughts.

Pascal, though, added a final thought. "You know, the plenary indulgence is a big motivator for the pilgrimage."

"The what?"

"An indulgence," said Pascal patiently. "The faith holds that those who travel the pilgrimage to its completion, not driving mind you, but travel the full way are pardoned of their sins."

"Like *all* their sins?" said Adele, eyebrows rising. She glanced toward Giam, wondering what sort of things Matthew and his brother might have wanted to clean their consciences of. Adele had never considered herself a particularly religious person. Her old mentor, Robert Henry, had been a man of faith, though, so she wasn't unfamiliar with some of the more characteristic activities involved.

94

Still, she'd never heard of the Camino de Santiago before… Certainly a religious overtone to all of this, now. The first victim had been a priest, the third victim was making a religious journey, and the second victim? She paused. She'd been found not far from an old abbey, but then again, Spain was filled with such sites.

Adele hissed through her teeth until they hurt. She nodded toward Giam and said, "Thank you for your time," before regaining her feet and moving toward where John had watched the whole exchange without so much as a comment.

As she walked away, listening to Pascal console Giam in his own language, Adele's thoughts were elsewhere. Were the religious overtones coincidental? Seemed a stretch.

John grunted as she drew near, peering out the window into the nighttime streets. He gave her a hopeful look. "Sleep?" he murmured.

Adele paused, but then shook her head. "Not yet. I—I need to look a few things up. But I think we might have a lead. A usable one this time."

CHAPTER NINETEEN

Adele's head hung low, her blonde hair drifting toward the keyboard as she leaned in, reading the small, cramped text back in the lobby of their hotel.

John was doing his best to stay awake, sitting across from her in the small hotel waiting room. A steaming cup of coffee sat next to him which he'd barely touched; yawning now, he leaned his head against his arm as he watched her across the table.

For a moment, as his big, brown eyes peered at her, Adele resisted an urge to smile. He looked a bit like a puppy, with his head curled up, watching her.

She reached across the table, patting the tall Frenchman on his large arm before returning her attention to her laptop.

"Anything?" John murmured. "Before I start sleepwalking?"

Adele hesitated. "I... You put that APB out yet?"

John snorted. "Pascal handled it. But what do you expect? Medium-height brown-haired men in Spain? They're going to pull every car over."

"Traveling alone," Adele said, quickly. "That's not nothing." She hesitated, rereading the article on her computer. "It's odd," she said, carefully. "You know where Father Fernando was killed?"

"The commune."

"Well... Saint-Jean-Pied-de-Port is considered a starting point for the 'French Way' of making the pilgrimage."

"French do this pilgrimage too?" John groaned. "That's another load of suspects."

"Yes, well... What if our killer is doing the pilgrimage also?"

John perked up and Adele leaned back in her chair, a satisfied look on her face.

"A murder pilgrim?" John murmured. "That might explain the connection. It isn't the victims themselves. It's where they are."

"Murder pilgrim?" she said, raising an eyebrow. "Not sure you should go throwing that cute little nickname around."

John shrugged, yawning again. "Sometimes my creative genius just strikes. I'm a victim of my own muse."

Adele rolled her eyes emphatically, but gave a little snort of laughter. "The only problem," she said, her tone sobering, "is the distance between the crime scenes. If the killer is doing the pilgrimage, he can't possibly move that fast on foot. But you're not allowed to use a car."

"Maybe he's not doing the pilgrimage. Maybe he's just hunting pilgrims."

"It's possible," she said, hesitantly. "The killer is moving too slowly to be doing it by car. But far too fast to be doing it on foot. I've been reading about the plenary indulgences too. And it's troubling."

John stared at her with bleary eyes, poking a large finger at his cup of coffee which was slowly going cold. "What about them?"

"I can't help but wonder what sort of person would need that kind of absolution. Someone very devout? Or maybe someone who knows they've done terrible things," Adele said, quietly.

John snorted. "In the case of our killer, that seems pretty obvious, doesn't it?"

Adele stared at him. She reached out, slowly lowering the lid of her computer. The stench of stale coffee hung over the hotel lobby. The clerk behind the desk had even gone, retreating into a back room. A little bell with a triangular placard read, *Ring for service.*

The two agents were alone in the small Spanish hotel. But there, Adele could feel something in her stomach twisting. She thought of a small man with a dull eye, thought of the pain he had inflicted. Thought of what he had done to her mother.

If he completed the pilgrimage, would he be absolved of everything? Of all the pain he had caused? Of all the people he had killed?

"What are you thinking?" John said, a bit more alert now, watching her.

"Is it fair for everyone to get absolved?"

John shrugged his shoulder. "I don't know about fair. Probably not up to me to make that call."

Adele shook her head. This answer wasn't satisfying. Some people were monsters. They deserved to be punished.

John, seemingly sensing they were getting off track, yawned again and crossed his arms behind his head in a posture of pure contentment. Still half yawning, he began his sentence, mouth wide, "All of this ends at some cathedral, yes?"

"At the shrine to St. James, and the cathedral," Adele said. "Yes. If our killer is doing the pilgrimage, eventually he will end up there"

"We could station out, wait for him to come to us."

"That could take days, weeks, depending on how fast he continues. Besides, if we wait for him to come to us, he'll leave a trail of bodies behind him."

Adele closed her eyes, thinking, but keeping quiet. One thing was for sure, she didn't want the killer to get to the cathedral. Petty, perhaps. Superstitious, maybe. But she didn't want him there. If she was right, if he had killed three people, maybe others they hadn't even heard about, then the last thing she felt a man like that deserved was absolution. She thought of Robert, of her mother, of the countless others. Their eyes often haunted her dreams. She couldn't do anything to bring them back. But the guilt of their passing wasn't something that could just be wiped away with a hike through the countryside. It wasn't something that could be brushed away.

No. She didn't want to wait for him at the cathedral. She wanted to catch him before. Before he could kill again. Before he could reach his destination.

***

Adele yawned for the second time in as many minutes, standing across from Agent Pascal as their Spanish correspondent typed into her phone and then muttered, "The APB has been adjusted. They'll be keeping an eye on the pilgrimage routes."

The three of them had reconvened in the hotel lobby. John looked better rested than Adele. She had stayed up another few hours, going over different routes through Northern Spain.

Now, standing in the lobby across from John and Pascal, Adele yawned again, trying to think straight. "Pascal," she said, "I was wondering if I could ask you something."

The Spanish agent nodded politely.

"Last night, I was going through the different routes our killer might be traveling. If he started at the commune, on the French Way, then he's been making quick time. Three days later he was in Santo Domingo de Silos. How could he be traveling that fast? It's not a car. If he'd been traveling by car, he could've done the whole thing in ten hours."

Agent Pascal smiled and patted the smaller woman on the shoulder. She turned toward the sliding glass doors, gesturing out at the sunlight, and said, "The pilgrimage is meant to be taken place under the sun. Without motorized vehicles. But that doesn't mean everyone plays exactly by the book. It isn't exactly forbidden, though sometimes frowned upon, but people use other means of transportation."

Adele hesitated. "What means?"

Pascal looked back, shrugging. "Nothing motorized. No vehicles. But maybe a cart. I've heard of someone doing it on a horse. Though, that one is disputed. And also, a lot of people do it by bike."

Adele smoothed her wrinkled suit. She had slept in her outfit, and hadn't woken up for her usual morning run. Which meant, inevitably, she was going to feel cranky throughout the day.

"Bike," John said. "That would account for the fast pace of travel, but not as fast as a car," he said. "Plus that would also mean our killer really is doing the pilgrim's travel."

Adele nodded slowly. It made sense. She could feel her excitement climbing. "All right," she said, "can we add that to the APB? Have them keep an eye out for cyclists in particular, who match the description the landlady gave us. Another thing," Adele continued, "last night he was *here*. If he really is traveling by bike, he probably got some sleep, but he's not going to be going much faster than fifteen or twenty-five kilometers per hour. Not over the long haul."

"True," said Pascal. "What would you like me to do with that?"

"That means, by this afternoon, he's not going to be able to get any further than Lugo."

John and Pascal both looked at her, impressed.

"I did the math twice," Adele explained. "Which means we need to notify businesses, hostels, restaurants, anything in the area. Give them a description of our guy, and keep an eye out for a biker. On top of that, we should send police to the area."

"On it," Pascal said.

John, yawning and stretching, said, "I take it that means we're headed to Lugo as well?"

Adele didn't even bother replying. They obviously had to cut the killer off before he got any further. If they reached Lugo before he did, they would be able to set a trap and spring it when he came pedaling through. Now, it was their turn to catch an unsuspecting target by surprise.

CHAPTER TWENTY

The man had a name, he just didn't like sharing it with people who were beneath the Lord's wisdom. A name was a powerful thing. The Messiah, once upon a time, had hidden his identity for years.

The father's was a noble cause. The man pedaled, his legs straining, his brow sweaty beneath the rising sun in the early morning. He didn't smile. Part of him wanted to. But another part of him balked at the trap of pleasure. The promises of this world could so easily ensnare the mind.

He continued pedaling. Last night had been unfortunate. He hadn't wanted to do that to Matthew. But the glutton deserved it.

He picked up the pace, catching a downward slope and riding it hastily toward the traffic lights at the bottom of the street; he could feel the wind against his face, cool and calming. Could feel the way his hair whipped about him. He would need to comb it when he stopped. There was no excuse for a shoddy appearance. His handkerchief still clutched against the handlebars.

He was so close. So very close. He would reach the cathedral tomorrow. The absolution would clean him completely. Now, he couldn't hold back the smile. He'd come so far, gone so long for this. As he flew down the hill, his mind on tomorrow's destination, a distant memory came fluttering back.

A loud voice shouted in a dormitory. Someone grabbed his leg, dragging him off the bed. Someone beat him. He winced as the memory played. He had known, from a very young age something in him had been wrong. The good Lord would cure it, though. He had spent his whole life trying to do the right thing. Gearing up for this very moment. St. James was watching. And soon, at the great man's burial site, things would be put right once more.

He pedaled a bit faster, determinedly fixated on the coming terrain as he sped down the hill, toward the traffic lights. Green lights ahead. Sometimes, the Lord just made a way. Around him, small, single-story buildings. Ahead of him, a crosswalk, with one pedestrian already reaching the sidewalk. Time seemed to go still as he reached the intersection at a breakneck pace.

As he sped through, beneath the green light, he heard a sudden screech of tires and looked sharply up, distracted from his memories.

A truck had run the red light, pulling toward him, having slammed on the brakes and spinning to the side. The back of the truck came careening toward his bicycle. He cursed, jerking to the side—his wheels twisted, and he toppled.

He managed to apply the brakes just enough to slow so the collision wasn't fatal.

The back of the truck caught the front of his bike, and he was sent flying. His leg caught the lip of the truck bed, slowing his progress a bit, but sending a jolting pain through his side. He hit the ground, rolling once, twice. Groaning, he blinked, dark spots dancing across his vision. Shakily, he tried to regain his feet, but found his legs threatening to give out.

For a moment, all he felt was pain and heat. Blood dripped along his hands were they'd scraped on the ground. His head hadn't hit anything. He should have been wearing a helmet. But he trusted the Lord. For good reason. He had survived.

He heard honking, followed by a voice shouting. "Are you okay, mister? Dear God. I'm so sorry. I didn't see you."

The father's hands were bleeding, but as he pushed up, leaving red stains against the asphalt, blinking, he found his vision adjusting once more. Groaning, with bolts of pain shooting down his back and along his thigh, he limped to his feet. He looked over his shoulder and realized his bicycle was one giant mangled mesh of spokes and metal and punctured rubber. The bike was totaled. The car had barely suffered a scrape. The driver was standing in front of the open door, shaking his head and holding his hands up in placation, apologizing profusely.

Repentance. He had done something wrong, running the red light. He could've killed someone. He nearly had. But now, he was repenting. The good Lord was fair.

The man dusted himself off, wincing, feeling his attention diverted once more toward the truck driver.

"Are you okay? I'm so sorry. I didn't see you. Look, here, let's trade information. I'll get you a new bike. I'm really sorry."

The man kept going on and on. How contrition ought to be. Still, the father had been enjoying himself too much. He smiled. The Lord was simply reminding him what life was. Suffering. The pain on his face, along his body, down toward his bruised knee and sprained ankle, would remind him of that. A good reminder. One he was grateful for. He limped a couple of steps toward his bike, a droplet of blood falling from his fingers and splashing against one of the spokes. Completely beyond repair. Beyond use.

The man in the truck was staring at him, stunned. "You look dazed. I'll call an ambulance. Again, I'm so sorry."

The father didn't reply. Speaking with others led to temptation.

The man who'd been driving the truck was still watching him hesitantly. "Should I get a name? Do you want to trade information?"

Finally, the father looked up, watching the truck driver. "I cannot lie to you," he said, hesitantly. "I'm not going to tell you my name."

"Hang on, mister, you need to. Look here, I can give you my insurance. I promise, I'll get you a new bike."

The truck driver took a step forward, but the father didn't wait to interact. He turned sharply on his heel and broke into a jog, wincing as he did, feeling hot lances of pain shoot up his right leg. He picked up the pace, increasing the pain. This was an appropriate response. The Lord had judged him. Judged him for pleasure. Judged him for getting too caught up in his own happiness. But eventually, when it was all said and done, he would be absolved of it all. He just needed another bike. He couldn't steal one. That would be inappropriate. A sin. He could feel the eyes of the truck driver behind him, glued to his shoulder blades as he continued to limp and jog away. More horns blared behind him at the truck blocking traffic. But he ignored it all, heading up a residential street, past an alley that smelled of refuse. He continued to run, seething, teeth gritted against the agony.

He needed another bike. Stealing was a sin. Perhaps he could barter for one. Or, perhaps, if he was fortunate, the Lord would provide another sign. Maybe someone who owned the bike. Maybe someone who would have to be punished. It wasn't wrong to take something from a sinner, was it? That wasn't the same as theft. No, that was justice. Yes. And he was a man of justice. He didn't like hurting people. Sometimes, though, the Lord made him.

He slowed a bit, gasping, wheezing, still in pain. One way or another, he needed to find another bike. He would reach that cathedral tomorrow. Nothing could stop him.

CHAPTER TWENTY ONE

Adele sat in the car with John, peering through the windshield, eyes glued to the streets outside Lugo. The air through the windows came fresh, sweet, carrying the fragrance of the natural vegetation around them. John was bored again, picking at some of the lint on his seat and throwing it out the window, watching as the breeze caught the fuzz and carried it away like dandelion fluff.

Adele tapped her fingers against the steering wheel, the same way the third victim's brother had at the cafe. Exhaustion still weighed heavy on her. The scent of coffee intermingled with that of the fragrance of the air. She was already on her third cup. For hours they'd sat here. Hours waiting. She glanced at the digital clock on the dash. It was nearly two in the afternoon.

"Maybe he's not coming," John said, as if sensing her frustration.

"He's coming," she snapped. "He has to be. This is going to be his next stop."

John seemed to know better than to argue with her when she got like this. She didn't mean to be unreasonable. She just hated sitting around and waiting. She checked her phone and then glanced at the radio, making sure it was connected. Occasionally she would pick up on chatter. Agent Pascal was in another vehicle, patrolling the street with officers. But no hits. Nothing on the APB. Nothing at all. They were turning up a giant blank.

Adele could feel her frustration mounting with every passing second. John pulled another tuft of lint, flicking it out the window again, and Adele watched the lint float on the breeze, carried lazily away.

"So we're looking for bikes," John said, hesitantly.

"We looking for anything," she growled. "Don't make my idea sound stupid. When you say it like that it sounds stupid."

"I wasn't trying to make it sound stupid."

"You said we're looking for bikes. Hear that? That sounds stupid."

"Adele, your idea isn't stupid. I was just wondering if that's why we've been sitting here for the last four hours."

Adele glared through the windshield.

"So what are we doing?"

"Looking for bikes," she muttered.

John rolled his eyes, throwing his hands toward the ceiling. He reached out, pulling open the door. "You know what," he said, "you need some food. And more coffee. Also, I wasn't going to say anything, but you're starting to smell."

Adele glared at him. "I am not. I didn't even run this morning."

John paused, sniffed at his own sleeve, and said, "Never mind. That might just be me. What do you want?"

"Food? I don't care. Anything. I could eat a horse."

John tapped his nose, slipping out of the car and pointed at her. "One horse coming up. Look, just sit tight. Lugo is far too big of an area for us to go door-to-door. We have no idea if he's going to be using this route."

"He has to," Adele said. "The pilgrimage routes are pre-mapped."

"According to Pascal, though, there is a lot of leeway," John reminded her. "You did your best. Now we just have to wait."

Adele crossed her arms, glaring through the windshield again. John, grateful to be doing something besides sitting around, shut the door and began to move toward a restaurant down the street. For a moment, she thought to call after him, to ask for a couple of meals. Her stomach twisted, growling. She realized she hadn't eaten anything in nearly twenty hours. Still, she had to focus. She glanced toward the phone again and then turned the radio up. Occasionally, over the designated station for the search, she heard Spanish. Agent Pascal had promised to translate if they found anything important.

Her phone suddenly blinked. Adele's reached out, snatching the device from the dash and lifting it. "Hello?"

Someone cleared their throat on the other end, and then, a crisp, clear voice said, "Agent Sharp?"

Adele's stomach fell. "Agent Paige?" Adele said, trying to hide her frustration. "I'm on a stakeout right now. Can I call you back later?"

"The reports you've been sending haven't been satisfactory, Agent Sharp. I'm just trying to help. What are you doing right now?"

"I'll report when I have something to report," she said. "We have an APB out in Lugo, looking for a pilgrim on bike matching a witness's description." She paused, inhaling through her nose and sighed. "I don't mean to be curt, but I haven't had much sleep."

Agent Paige on the other end sighed. "You're not taking care of yourself?"

Adele scoffed. "No, that's not what I'm saying. Look, I'm trying my best. Don't call back." She hung up. Adele stared at her hand, a slow sense of horror coming over her. Had she just hung up on Agent Paige? The woman was acting in the executive's stead on this case. Not to mention performance reviews, and Adele had just hung up on her.

Adele massaged her temples, muttering a series of oaths beneath her breath. So stupid. So very stupid. Still, she didn't have time to play these games. She jammed her phone back into her pocket, determined to ignore it if it rang again. She would just have to deal with Agent Paige later. Her stomach grumbled, and she glanced out the windshield toward where John was entering the restaurant. If he brought back pickles she was going to scream.

As her eyes wandered toward the lint-covered seat which John had been picking at, she noticed something else. The sound of a ringing phone. And there, where it had fallen from his pocket, jammed beneath the seat, John's cell phone.

She stared. Was Agent Paige calling Renee now, to reprimand Adele?

Or was it something else?

The phone continued to ring, and Adele just stared at her partner's device. She knew she shouldn't. It wasn't really her business. She didn't want to be the prying girlfriend. But...

She sat frozen for a moment, just watching as the phone blinked, flashing blue, and the ring tone emanated in the car. It was warm, even with the windows rolled down. She was bored. For hours they'd been sitting there. Plus, she was downright curious. For weeks now, John had received mysterious phone calls. The last few days they'd intensified. Who kept calling him?

She wasn't going to answer. The phone rang a fourth time. She just wanted to assuage some of her curiosity. She reached down, delicate, barely touching the phone. Somewhere, in her subconscious, she determined that if she didn't hold the phone, at least not too tightly, it didn't count as prying. A single letter on the phone. No name, the number was hidden. But the phone displayed the contact. A letter: "B."

B? Did Adele know a *B*?

She winced. Her fingers still grazed the cold metal of the phone. She knew she should've ignored it. The device rang again.

Despite herself, despite her best instincts, and determined to blame sleep deprivation if anyone ever asked, she picked up the phone, placed it to her ear, and said, "Hello?"

She waited. Someone breathed heavily on the other end. And then, a woman's voice. A young woman. Maybe Adele's age. "John?"

"No, I'm sorry, he's not here right now. Who is this?"

"Who is *this*?"

"I'm John's friend. He's not here. Are you the one who keeps calling him?"

The woman on the other end snorted. "I should've known he'd shacked up with some floozy."

Adele bristled.

"Well, Ms. Mysterious, if you'd be so kind, tell that giant lump it would be nice," she said, her tone biting, "if he could maybe take a couple of minutes out of his very important busy schedule to spend time with his daughter."

Adele sat, stunned. "Hang on, his *daughter*?"

"Yes, dear. And let me warn you. Renee, he'll cycle through you like most women. Did he meet you at a bar last night? At a club a couple of days ago? Don't believe him. He's not the sort to stick around. Trust me, I know. And our daughter, she also knows."

The woman hung up.

Adele stared at the phone. At the *B*. The phone had turned from blue to white. The call disconnected.

She wanted to scream. John had a daughter? Of course, she had always known Renee had a womanizing past—she had been careful, cautious with him. But they'd known each other for longer than just a couple of days. And he had stuck around, to her astonishment. She'd thought he was turning over new leaf. But now this. How on earth did he have a daughter, and more importantly, why hadn't she ever heard about it?

Just then, the door opened. Adele looked up, startled, dropping the phone where it hit the cushioned chair. The scent of burgers and fries filled the car. John was grinning, extending a bag of food, but then froze. His smile turned to a frown. He glanced from Adele, down to his phone, and then his eyes darted back up again. His eyes widened briefly, and he stared, stunned, seemingly waiting for her to speak first.

"You have a *daughter*?" Adele said, grabbing the bag of food if only to take it out of his hand.

John swallowed. He hesitated, and didn't slip into the car, leaving the door open and resting his hands on the roof. He leaned down, peering into the cab. "Were you going through my phone?"

"Yes. I was. Very much. Now my turn: *Do you have a daughter?*"

"You shouldn't go through my stuff."

"You got a call. I answered it. Sorry. Now, just one more time in case you didn't hear me: you have a *daughter*?" Adele could feel her heart pounding. The paper bag in her hand, heavy with junk food, seemed unimportant now. She didn't feel hungry anymore. If anything, she felt sick to her stomach.

"Adele, look, it's not what you think."

"Have you been seeing someone else?"

"Christ, no," he snapped, adamantly. His hand slammed against the roof. He shook his head violently. "I haven't seen Bernadette in nearly ten years. She keeps hassling me. I don't want anything to do with her. I haven't been seeing anyone else. I swear on my life. I swear it on everything."

Adele let out a loose, strained breath. Delicately, she placed the bag of food on the dash. She brushed some dust from the steering wheel, absentmindedly wiping her hand off on her suit pants, which were still horribly wrinkled. She looked back up at John. "Why didn't you tell me you had a daughter?"

"It was ten years ago. She's not in my life. I never see her."

"But you didn't tell me."

John closed his eyes for a moment, rubbing at his face before returning his hand to the roof of the car, still leaning in, half in the vehicle and half out.

"Shit," he said. "I didn't think it mattered. Like I said, I don't see them. Bernadette made it clear, she didn't want anything to do with me. It's only been in the last couple of years—she's had some financial troubles and now she wants to get in touch. It's all to make a child-support case against me."

"John, I don't care about that. That's between you and them. I'm talking about us. Why didn't you tell me at least?"

John hesitated, scratching his chin, and sighed. "You know what, because honestly, I wasn't sure we were going to go this far. Yeah, there, I said it. I didn't think it was worth telling you, because I didn't think you wanted anything to do with me. You played cold for a while. And by the time things started to warm, I felt like it wasn't important. Because it isn't. You're important to me, Adele. They aren't."

Adele wasn't sure how she felt about this. She didn't like the idea of John discarding his daughter as if she didn't even matter. She thought of the Sergeant. She thought of their own strained relationship. John was a harsh man also. He had his soft side, but it was hidden deep. More importantly, however, she didn't like that he hadn't told her. It was as if he wasn't taking things seriously. Was she just another throwaway for him? Why wouldn't he tell her something this important if she really mattered? Unless this was all some big game. Maybe he was just toying with her. He'd been taking calls, lying about them. It would've been so easy, so many times, just to mention it.

"Do you care about this?" she said, waving a hand from her to him and back. "Or doesn't this matter either?"

John snorted, spitting off to the side. "That's not fair. How is that fair?"

"I don't know. But you're the one saying you didn't think we'd get this far. Now that we're here, you haven't said anything about your daughter—that's a big deal. Clearly you don't care enough to tell me these things."

John's tone darkened. "I *refuse* to feel bad about this. I didn't think it mattered. That's not my fault. You don't tell me things either. You have a past. I don't go prying into it. I have never asked you about half the things you've been up to. Your mother? I let you talk about it at your own pace. Because I know it's painful. That was ten years ago also. Would you rather I just bombard you with questions about her? How it felt? If it hurt when she died? If you liked the way it changed your career? No? That would be prying. It would be rude. It's none of my business. If you want to tell me, I'm happy to hear. But it's more important that we just do *us*. Not baggage from a decade ago."

"It's not the same thing! Don't bring up my mother."

He jabbed a finger at her. "Exactly. See. It hurts. It doesn't matter—"

"It absolutely matters," she snapped. "You know about it. That doesn't mean I have to tell you every little detail. But you know about it. I didn't know you had a daughter. You refused to tell me."

John threw up his hands, placing them against his head and staring at the sky for a moment. He inhaled deeply, his large chest heaving.

For a moment, Adele just stared at him. She wanted to say more, but what was there to say? Clearly, he didn't take the relationship seriously enough to speak with her about something this essential. Clearly she had been mistaken about him all along. Or maybe she was overreacting. She was hungry, tired, stressed, and surrounded with bodies falling like flies. Maybe this wasn't the proper time to speak with John. But then again, perhaps that was just an excuse.

She let out a long sigh, staring at where John was still glaring into the sky.

"I don't know what to say," she murmured, facing the open door.

John didn't reply, still stretching, ignoring her.

Where could they even go from here? Adele didn't know. He'd been lying about the calls, too. She hadn't expected Agent Renee to be perfect. She would've been a fool to assume that. But he'd been lying.

108

He'd been secretive. He didn't take their relationship seriously. Was it really her job to fix all his own personal baggage? It was one thing to empathize, another to enable. Adele had to work through her own shit. For decades she'd been forced to. She'd even done therapy. But what about John? He thought everyone was going to leave. That everyone would die or abandon him. And so he abandoned them first.

Just because she understood it, and felt sympathy for it, didn't mean she had to endure it.

The scent of the hamburgers and fries smelled stale for a moment. Adele wanted to slam the door shut on John and drive away, leaving him behind. But she'd already hung up on Paige. Perhaps she wasn't in the most rational, decision-making frame of mind.

Just then, a voice crackled over the radio. Adele jerked, her attention shifting, getting emotional whiplash as she tried to focus.

She pressed a button and said, "Yes, Agent Pascal?"

The voice crackled again and said, "Agent Sharp? Renee? We have an innkeeper nearby. He says someone fitting the description of our suspect recently checked in."

Adele stared, feeling her mouth dry. "Was this person driving a bicycle?"

Another crackle. "Affirmative. They just checked in five minutes ago. What would you like me to do?"

Adele swallowed back the emotions burbling through her, trying to think for a moment, and then said, "Wait for us. Please text the address. We'll meet you there." Things with John would have to wait. She was still irritated, still frustrated, but she had to compartmentalize at least for the moment.

"Get in," she called out. John ducked down, looking at her again, his expression indeterminable. "We got a hit," she said. "Get in, buckle up. Let's go."

CHAPTER TWENTY TWO

The painter's body hadn't quite adjusted to the time difference between Paris and San Francisco. He held a hand to his mouth, yawning where he stood in the darkness of the small row of trees outside the apartment complex. It had been easy enough to climb the wall and the side alley, slipping through the garden paths to take a seat on the bench facing the apartment. Now, he had a perfect view of the second-floor window.

The painter played with his new toy, passing it from one hand to the other, spinning it once, twice, feeling the heft, the balance. Stray strands of moonlight caught the blade, reflecting off the edge.

He glanced down at the bench, where splinters scattered. Gouge marks in the wood displayed where he had tested the sharpness of his new toy.

It had been a sacrifice, leaving his favorite equipment back in Paris, but he hadn't wanted to raise any questions. Already, the authorities were on the lookout for him. Already, his face was likely circulating throughout airports and terminals. Still, he had come this far, and whether his equipment was faulty or not, he would see the masterpiece through. Thankfully, the knife he had picked up from the curio shop would do nicely.

A light flickered in the second floor window. The trees around him swayed and shook, trembling in the faint wind. The gate at his back stood resolute and solid, locked. The sandstone walls were high, not unassailable, especially not for someone with his experience, but intimidating to any small-time crook who might pass by. He wrinkled his nose, feeling a jolt of disgust. He hated criminals and thieves. Scumbags—the dregs of society.

He winced, testing his bad leg as he got to his feet, standing in front of the bench beneath the trees. Slowly, he pocketed his knife, leaving his hand against the bone hilt.

A shadow passed across the window. He smiled, watching as a man with curly brown hair brushed his teeth. Curtains open, lights on. The perfect spectacle.

People were so inattentive.

"Hello, my dear," he murmured. "You look quite stunning tonight."

The man in the window couldn't hear him. Didn't see him. Didn't realize he had an audience. Which only made things more pleasurable.

The painter giggled to himself, a high-pitched, creaking sound. He watched some more as the shadow disappeared out of sight, likely going to spit the toothpaste into a sink.

He liked watching them. For hours now, well into the night, he'd stayed in the shadows of the garden, just watching. Enjoying the view. It was a delightful thing. He continued to watch as the lights suddenly clicked off.

Someone was going to bed—a late night for his new friend. A wealthy man, judging by the apartment in San Francisco. Judging by the career profile he'd found on the Internet. A wealthy man with no clue.

The lights were off. A lesser artist might have made their move. But half the fun was the wait. Watching. Attentive to every detail. He pulled the knife from his pocket again, slowly lowering back to the bench. He was in no rush. His friend would go to sleep soon. He traced the blade through the cuts in the bench. A familiar swirling pattern. One of his favorites. A difficult thing to do without completely breaking the skin too deeply and causing the cracks to mesh together. He had tried it first on Elise. Adele's mother had howled so delightfully. He could still remember the pitch of her screams, like the falsetto crooning of some soloist. He had always fancied himself a painter first, but now, the more he spent time perfecting his craft, the more he thought about moving into other avenues of creative expression. A conductor, too, perhaps?

He could collect the pitch of their shouts and cries of agony. Perhaps record them, make something out of them. Some sort of music.

He smiled in delight at the thought. This was how he always stayed on top of his game; creative genius didn't rest. He had more ideas for beauty and he had years left.

Besides, all of this was going to culminate in a final masterpiece now. He knew how she would react when she found out. In the end, this had to end face to face. Far sooner than she might have thought. Much, much sooner.

Time passed but he didn't notice, still sitting on the bench, still biding his time, smiling toward the second-floor window. Still dark. No lights, no movement, no witnesses. An audience would come soon enough but even they were absent for now. This part of the creative process happened in private.

He gave a soft little sigh and then slowly got to his feet. He shot a look back at the bench, at the swirling pattern. A practice scratch before the big reveal. Would he do something with the man's eyes? Sometimes he liked leaving them untouched. Other times he felt this was dishonest to the piece.

Leaves crunched beneath his feet as he limped off the grass onto the cobblestone path to the front doors of the gated complex.

Three hours ago he'd already memorized the code for the building. People weren't very good at guarding their secrets.

Even with a dull eye, he had eyesight like a hawk in the other.

He entered the code he had seen that cute young businesswoman use a couple of hours before. The door buzzed, and he stepped in

He approached the stairs, still moving carefully, slowly, with an air of excitement. The anticipation was nearly as beautiful as the final product. He took the stairs slowly, moving up one at a time. Already, in his mind's eye, he played out what would come next. It always started the same way. Shock, disbelief, fury, and then terror. This last part was his favorite.

He reached the top of the stairs and curled around the banister, approaching the door facing the east side of the building. He didn't knock. Though, in the past, he had done just that to gain entry with some of his earlier pieces.

Now, his skills were more honed.

He examined the door for second, his gaze fixated on the lock.

High-security, as he'd assumed. Instead of trying the door, he moved, heading toward the window overlooking the street. The foyer window stared down at the park bench where he'd been sitting. He opened the window, felt the breeze against his face, blinking.

He had a small form, like that of a child. It didn't help when it came to physical acts. But when it came to slipping into small spaces, it had served him well in the past. Now, as he opened the window, he slipped out, pulling himself onto the outside of the building. He gripped the windowsill as he leveraged his body against the painted wall.

If anyone had been watching, they would've seen him start to move like a monkey, hand over hand, along the drainpipe and gutter dangling from the roof. He moved until he dangled over the window he'd been watching. He had traced the path with his eyes for the last few hours, rehearsing it in his mind. He didn't even need to look as he extended his hand and caught the trellis. Then, with a show of strength that might have surprised the uninitiated, he lowered his small form until he was dangling one-armed from a wooden trellis, facing the dark window. The curtains were still open.

He smiled, faintly catching his reflection in the glass due to the moon. Like a small monkey, hanging over the ledge in the search for food. Unlike a monkey, he wouldn't eat what he found within his haunt. No, consumption would ruin the work. He knew some artists who liked to consume their pieces, but he'd always found the practice distasteful.

The painter landed on the sill, bracing himself against the frame and the jutting concrete around the window. The pressure of his hands kept his body lodged. With one hand extended, holding himself in place in front of the window, the other moved toward the frame. He pushed, but the window didn't budge. He frowned, slipping his hand into his pocket and withdrawing his new toy. He wiggled the knife between the cracks of the window and the frame. He jerked it a bit and then felt something *click*. The knife tapped against the metal latch. Tongue inside his cheek, one hand still pressing his body against the window, a foot jutting to the concrete protrusion to hold him in place, he maneuvered the knife. The doors would be secure. The people weren't very creative nowadays. They would lock themselves in a mansion with bolts and security systems and all manner of chains and electronic locks. And then they would leave glass windows all around. Windows could be broken. *Should* be broken. Could be opened. This was how he'd taken Robert Henry.

His knife moved. The latch lifting. He grinned to himself, shimmying his knife back and forth until the gap widened. Slowly, he maneuvered his small fingers in the gap and pulled. Ever so quietly, the window opened, and he slipped into the second-story apartment, leaving the night to enter the apartment.

No one saw him. No one screamed. Perfect.

He dusted himself off, adjusting his sweater, pulling the hood up and tugging on the drawstrings. He scanned the apartment. Sparse, with a couple of boxes in one corner suggesting the tenant still hadn't unpacked. A single couch sat beneath the window, and he slid past this, walking quietly past the kitchen.

For a moment he just stood in the middle of the room, enjoying the carpet beneath his feet, the sense of quiet accomplishment. The window was still mostly closed. He hadn't needed to open it much to escape.

Being small came with benefits.

He moved down the hall, resisting the urge to whistle. Sometimes he liked to make a sound, if only to alert his new friends. Fear got the blood going. Panic and adrenaline got the muscles taut. All of it made for a better canvas. He had to be mindful of that sort of thing, like a painter mixing paints. Acrylic or not. Water-based or otherwise. It was up to him to choose his canvas medium. Now, he didn't want the blood flowing too much. This masterpiece, in his mind, didn't need that much red. And if the canvas was loose, limp, he would be able to contort it better. This time, the shapes he had in mind needed a more pliable medium; he clutched his knife in one hand, moving down the hall. On his right, a bathroom. Then a closet.

Which only left one door at the far end of the hall.

He approached it, smiling to himself as he did. He reached for the door handle, careful, patient. Then he turned the handle, pushing the door opened with the faintest of creaks.

A bed. A lump beneath sparse blankets. No movement. The quiet droning of a fan on the desk, and another one on the ceiling. The room was cold. And the painter could feel his teeth begin to hurt from the frigidity. His bones were weaker than most. He frowned as he stepped into the room, still quietly, moving toward the lump on the bed. The man didn't even seem to react. The painter frowned. Some of the fun was lost without a struggle. Part of the enjoyment was the difficulty. He sighed, standing in front of the bed, knife tapping against his upper thigh.

The lump beneath the blankets shifted a bit, pulling a comforter over his head.

The painter sighed a bit louder, clearing his throat.

The man beneath the blanket didn't see him.

The painter crossed his arms, staring, unblinking, watching the man beneath the blankets. Then he began to whistle, a faint, soft tune.

Like twittering birds in the night. He stood at the foot of the man's bed, whistling.

The lump beneath the blankets shifted again, groaning, muttering. And then the movement stiffened. The painter smiled. He wondered what the man was thinking, as his sleepy self roused to consciousness. His eyes were still closed, but the way he had frozen suggested he was now aware someone was in his room. The whistling, the strange, itching sensation at the base of one's spine when they knew they weren't alone where they should have been.

The man beneath the blanket turned suddenly, jolting upright, eyes wide like pale moons in the dark. He stared, not quite believing his eyes, and then began to scream.

But the painter moved fast. He darted forward, snatching one of the pillows as he moved and jamming it against the man's face. His knife flashed, down once, down twice. Then he backed off. He wanted the man to fight, to struggle.

"Come on," the painter said, his voice soft and lilting. "Let's play.

114

What would you like to do next? Don't scream. That didn't work. Maybe you should try to run. Yes, that's it. Go on, I'll wait. You start. Let's see if I can get to you before you get to the door."

The man on the bed was gasping, bleeding. He didn't seem to realize he'd been stabbed, though. He frantically reached for the lamp by his bedside, lifting it and throwing it at the painter. It missed. The wounded, sleep-deprived fellow tried to push off the bed, shoving toward the door. He made two steps before the painter tripped him. Far faster, far more nimble. He laughed, chuckling. The man tried to scream again, but the painter put the pillow against his face once more, making a shushing sound. He reached out, holding a knee against the man's chest while holding the pillow to his face. With one hand he stroked the curly hair. "There, there," he murmured. "It's scary, isn't it? You should be scared. I'm going to do horrible things to you for hours. There's nothing you can do to stop it. Would you like to try again? All right, let's go another time. I'm going to let you up now. You could try to tackle me. You're stronger. Or maybe you can run again. Which one? Either? You know what, don't tell me. I like surprises."

The painter stepped back, lifting the pillow. The man on the ground gasped, trying to scream again, then bolted toward the door.

The painter let him get a head start, grinning, and then he broke into a sprint after his new friend. This was always fun. He'd forgotten how much fun. Now, as he chased down the hall, his footsteps thumping in the wake of his bleeding friend, he felt the familiar thrill of sheer exhilaration.

CHAPTER TWENTY THREE

Adele was driving. A nice change of pace given the last two excursions with Pascal's and John's usual speeds. Then again, she was pushing limits too. As she ripped through the streets, heading in the direction of the address for the inn with the APB hit, she shot a sidelong glance at John, who was glaring solemnly out the windshield. She didn't know what to make of it all. She didn't even know how to process this new information. He had a kid. He hadn't told her. He hadn't thought it was worth mentioning. Still, now wasn't the time to think about this.

They raced down the streets as the GPS chirped instructions.

"I have a name," came a crackling voice over the radio. "A name. Innkeeper just got back. How far are you?"

Adele cursed, glancing at the GPS. "Five minutes," she replied. "Are you there yet?"

"Almost," Pascal returned. "Want the name?"

Adele nodded, then realized she couldn't be seen. "Yes, Pascal, what's the suspect's name?"

"I just got off the phone with the innkeeper. He says the man's name is Santiago Segura."

Adele wrinkled her nose. "Santiago Segura? Are you sure?"

"As sure as I can be," said Pascal.

To his credit, John didn't wait for an instruction. His phone was already in his hand, as he began to hastily enter the information into their database

For a moment, still racing through the streets, heading in the direction of the inn, everything just passed in silence. Then John looked up. "Santiago Segura?" he said quickly.

Adele nodded.

"This look like our guy?"

John thankfully seemed to be willing to put their differences behind them for now in service of the case. She looked over as he held out his phone. She stared at a mug shot. A man with a buzzed head and a beaklike nose. He was glaring into the camera.

"I guess the bristle is brown—matching the landlady's description. Maybe he's grown his hair out now. Height looks average. Why does he have a mug shot?"

John pulled his phone back, scrolling through the file. He inhaled sharply and said, "Looks like he was involved in a wrongful death case—charged with murder. His brother-in-law. Some dispute over a restaurant."

Adele shot a look at John. "He killed someone?"

"That's what the prosecution tried to say."

"So why isn't he in jail?"

John shook his head. "I guess they couldn't get a conviction. He was arrested, hence the mug shot, but they let them go. Found not guilty."

Adele felt her heart hammer. She picked up the pace, drawing close to Agent Pascal levels of speed.

Santiago Segura fit the description. Dark hair, dark eyes, average height, riding a bicycle on the pilgrimage route. He had also once been arrested for murder. Cleared or not, that gave him a far deeper connection to the case.

Briefly, Adele considered what she'd read about the plenary indulgence. Absolution for anything. For all the crimes and sins one might have committed. She had wondered at the time what sort of sin would prompt someone to travel so far. Murder would fit the list, wouldn't it?

Was Mr. Segura feeling guilty about the murder of his brother-in-law? Was that why he was traveling the pilgrimage?

If he was killing along the way, out of a sense of sick pleasure or compulsion, the absolution would clear him from that as well.

Adele gritted her teeth, hands gripping the steering wheel as she followed the GPS as it chirped instructions. She screeched down a side street, weaving through the two lanes of traffic.

It all fit. In a creepy, twisted sort of way. Why these victims, though?

"Think it's our guy?" John muttered.

Adele said, "I plan to ask him in person. Hang tight, it's just up ahead."

***

John hated sitting passenger side. For one, Adele drove like his grandma. For another, it gave him nothing to do but think. He hated thinking. Thinking was distracting from *doing*. Now, though, as Adele made a beeline toward the parking lot of the roadside inn, the flashing neon sign pointing the way, he could feel his thoughts trying to catch up with his emotions.

He shot a glance at Adele out of the corner of his eye, and then looked back at the road.

Clearly she hadn't understood. He wasn't always good at phrasing things. He knew what he meant, but when he spoke, sometimes the words just got jumbled. Other times his own stupid temper got in the way.

Was Adele right to be mad?

Why was it any of her business that he had a kid? It wasn't like he saw the kid. He wasn't even allowed to for the first few years. And now that his ex was down on her luck, she wanted financial support. He knew what she was trying to do. By getting him time with his child, she would be able to go to a judge to make a case for child support.

He could see it coming from a mile away.

He glanced at Adele again, back out the window. It had been fun seeing the way she had spoken with her father back at the apartment. He was a rough man, a tough one. But Adele clearly loved him.

Things hadn't been smooth between them, either.

Maybe he was taking it out on the wrong person. But what if his kid didn't want to see him?

John twisted uncomfortably in his seat, staring as Adele hit her turn signal, merged, and began to pull into the driveway outside the inn.

He felt poised, ready to move, but at the same time, he realized he'd uncovered something he didn't want to know. The discomfort he was feeling was only in part from sitting in a car with Adele. Another part of him wondered if this last thought was true. What if she didn't want to see him? What if his daughter would show up a couple of times, think he was some weird loser, and leave? It wasn't like he was father of the year. He hadn't even been in her life for a decade. Why would she want to see him now?

He regretted neglecting her. He hadn't ever really wanted kids. He hadn't thought it would be safe for him to have them. If anything, he would just ruin them. Didn't Bernadette see that? Besides, he'd only really seen her for a week. A one-night stand had turned into a week of lovemaking. It had been fun. And then the kid had come. Why was it that everyone thought he had to suddenly care for the kid just because he'd slept with someone? He slept with a lot of people. If all of them popped out kids that didn't mean he'd suddenly become a father figure.

His insides wormed again.

He cursed beneath his breath, staring through the window as Adele pulled sharply into a parking spot and flung open the door.

He was already mid-motion, pushing open his own door. This was why he hated thinking. It only left him feeling guilty. No, he didn't have an answer for any of it. He was no one's father. He wasn't good at that sort of thing. He would just ruin the girl. And, more likely, and perhaps a bit more honestly, he was terrified she would want nothing to do with him after meeting him. Maybe it was best for everyone involved he just stayed away.

He flung open the door, hurrying alongside Adele as they moved hastily up the steps.

Agent Pascal was already waiting for them in the lobby with two police officers at her side. A frazzled-looking man was standing behind the counter, pointing up the stairs and jabbering something quickly.

He lowered his hand and then pointed toward the far end of the hall, up the stairs and then down again.

Pascal said, "He's got a room upstairs, but he is currently in the dining hall, alone," she said, hurriedly.

The flash of lights behind him through the open door illuminated the slick tiled ground.

John growled as he took the lead, hastening around the stairs in the indicated direction of the chow hall.

Adele followed close behind, doing her best to keep up. But John put on an extra burst of speed. He didn't need anyone to hold him back.

He reached the swinging double doors to the dining hall, waited a second, and then kicked open the door, shouting at the top of his lungs, "Hands up, DGSI!"

A man was sitting in the back of the small space, near some curtains which had been thrown open to allow the sun into the room. He took a long sip of soup, lowered his spoon, and then slowly, with baleful eyes, looked up. He had brown hair instead of a buzzed head now. He had the same beak-shaped nose from his mug shot. Mr. Segura glanced from one of them to the next, and then with a bored expression returned his attention to the soup. He took another sip.

Adele and John, with Pascal behind them, moved then, weapons raised. "Hands up, get away from the table," John shouted.

The man sighed, taking another sip of soup. Then he stood up, holding a steak knife in one hand. He twirled the knife, once, twice, and called out, "What is this about?" he said in French.

"Get down!" John shouted.

The man looked around at them, blinking. It was almost as if he couldn't sense fear. He didn't jerk back, didn't panic. He looked bored more than anything. The guns didn't earn anything more than a passing glance and a snort. Mr. Segura lowered his spoon and lifted the knife to pick at his teeth.

John and Adele circled the table. Pascal stayed where she was, blocking the doors.

"Mr. Segura," Adele said, firmly. "You need to put the knife down. Hands up."

He picked at his teeth again, frowned, dug a bit deeper. A faint stream of blood poured from his gums down his white teeth. But then he gave a click of satisfaction and removed the knife, a small brown strand of meat caught on the end.

"The steak was like rubber," the man said, shaking his head. He made a tutting sound and then placed the knife back on the table. He raised his hands, and, in the air of a man practiced with law enforcement, he went to his knees, hands still on his head, then down to his belly.

Seconds later, John and Adele were both on him. John went for the cuffs, and Adele began rapidly checking his pockets.

"Mr. Segura, stay down," John cautioned. "Don't move."

"I will not," the man replied in French, through a mouthful of carpet. "I really must commend you. That was only two seconds to cuff me. The last guy who did it took five. I keep track for fun."

John growled, beginning to lift the man as Adele pulled another knife out of the fellow's pocket, placing it on the table.

"Mr. Segura, you're coming in for questioning," John snapped.

CHAPTER TWENTY FOUR

Adele didn't know what to make of this new suspect. He seemed emotionless. Completely devoid of any fear or concern for his own well-being. When they had cuffed him, he hadn't protested. When John had pushed him into the back of the sedan, he hadn't protested. Now, as John roughly dragged his handcuffed arms forward, looping them through the slots in the interrogation room table, he went along compliantly, making no move to defend himself or resist.

Adele watched the strange fellow. His head wasn't buzzed as it had been in his mug shot. He looked older now. Maybe in his forties, or even fifties. A thin speckle of gray beneath the brown suggested the true color of his hair. He had a silver mustache, which didn't match the rest of his hair. Mr. Segura watched the two of them as John pushed away and then settled in the chair across the interrogation room table.

Agent Pascal was still talking with the local area sergeant in the hall outside, maintaining access to the room for now. Clearly, by the sound of raised voices through the door, this portion of Spain didn't much like CNI commandeering one of their rooms.

But Adele would leave the politics to the locals. She had a case to solve.

"Why did you have a knife on you?" Adele said, firmly.

Santiago spoke French easily enough. It sounded like it might have been his first language. Though it was difficult to tell. He hesitated, but then said, "Which knife? One of them I was using to pick steak out of my teeth."

"The other one," Adele replied. "Seven inches. That's not a knife for utility. It is for hurting things."

"Or protecting," the man said, nonchalantly. "But in my case, you're right. The knife is meant for hurting things."

Adele and John shared a look. She cleared her throat, hesitant. "So you admit it?"

He smiled faintly. It wasn't a pandering, teasing sort of expression. It wasn't mocking, or even deranged. It simply seemed like an authentic, genuinely sad smile. He shrugged once. "I was going to hurt myself. I considered for a while if I ought not. But it seemed like the right thing to do at the time."

121

John shifted uncomfortably in his chair, the metal legs scraping against the floor. Adele leaned back, frowning beneath the bright lights above. "You're going to hurt yourself?"

"Indeed."

"Do you hurt yourself often?"

"No. Not intentionally. I was going to kill myself." He said it like he was commenting on the weather. Again, his emotions seemed completely disassociated from his words. He looked around the room and glanced at the clock, as if wondering how long this would take.

"Are you all right?" Adele said, carefully. "Do you know where you are?"

The man glanced back at her and smiled again. "Yes, I'm sorry, Detective. I'm not trying to be difficult."

"Maybe you can help me understand."

The man nodded. "Certainly. I'd love to try at least. How can I help you?"

"I have a few questions, but maybe we can start with the *killing yourself* part." Adele tried to keep her tone neutral, but it was a difficult thing to do. Something was clearly off about this man—he spoke like in a dream, as if nothing mattered, without a single ounce of self-preservation.

The man wagged his head dutifully. He sat straight-backed, making no motion with his wrists, as if worried he might scuff the chains binding him. "It's nothing," he said, hesitantly. "Absolution. I was walking the pilgrimage, you know. The French Way."

"You speak French."

"I am half French."

"I see."

"Do you believe in absolution, Agent?"

"What do you mean?"

"Do you think someone can be absolved of the sins in their past?"

"Are you talking about the man you killed?"

He hesitated and began to shake his head, but then stopped. "I wasn't found guilty of that."

"And yet your conscience seems to weigh heavy." Adele shrugged. "People with clean consciences don't tend to feel guilty enough to kill themselves."

"Who said it was guilt?" he said.

"I can't be sure. Maybe you can help me understand. Why did you want to kill yourself?"

"Not *did*. Do. I probably still will. I thought about it for a long time," he said, continuing in a conversational tone, entirely devoid of emotion. Respectful, polite, but cold. "I walked the pilgrimage for a bit; I felt like perhaps it might cleanse my soul. Maybe make me feel better. But it doesn't seem right, does it?"

Adele hesitated. She didn't say anything, allowing him to continue. Was he confessing?

"It doesn't seem right that one could get off without punishment. Some things even punishment won't fix. Like a dead person."

"Your brother-in-law?" Adele prompted.

"Yes. He was."

"No one else?"

"Should there be?"

"You tell me." Adele crossed her arms, her suit wrinkling as she stared at the man—a strange mass of contradictions, of oddities.

"I don't know," he said, hesitantly, with a long sigh. His silver mustache and brown hair seemed a mismatch, similar to the words he spoke and the emotions he displayed.

"Have you killed anyone else?" Adele said, bluntly.

The man looked at her. Instead of seeming shocked, or annoyed, or angry, he simply said, "I don't think so."

"Most people know if they've killed anyone."

He shook his head. "I don't really know anything anymore. If it isn't sinners who deserve absolution, then no one does. People who deserve forgiveness have to call it something else. It's not forgiveness if it is deserved. But it's not justice if it's overlooked. If you can just get away with anything you do, what's to stop you from killing or raping or stealing?"

"You've done these things?" Adele said.

The man continued as if she hadn't spoken. "What's the point? Why try so hard if you can say a little prayer, go on a long walk, and get away with it? It doesn't make sense, does it?"

Adele shrugged. "I don't know. It's not my area of expertise."

The man sighed, passing a hand through his hair, forced to duck his head so he could reach it with the handcuff.

When he looked up again, he just looked tired. "I don't have the answers, Agent. I don't know what you're looking for. If you tell me, maybe I can be of help."

"We're looking into murders," Adele said. She was surprised at how straightforward she replied to the question. Then again, he was being nothing but straightforward in return.

The man nodded. "I see. And I might have done them, is that it?"

"Did you?"

"Kill someone? When?"

Three times in the last four days," Adele said, quietly. "On the same pilgrimage path that you're taking now."

He nodded and said, "I see. For what it's worth, no, I haven't killed anyone. Not in a long time." He gave another long sigh, Adele glimpsed, beneath the facade of calm, a roiling sea of emotion behind the man's eyes. She glimpsed pain—a pain she was familiar with. The pain of regret. Of anger and sadness. And also she glimpsed the self-loathing that would prompt a man to buy a knife to use on himself.

Adele sighed, getting slowly to her feet. She said, "I'll be back." John glanced at her, frowning, and she gave a faint gesture for him to follow.

The two of them rose and exited the interrogation room, moving out into the hall. As the door began to close, Adele glimpsed Santiago one last time. He just sat there, stony-faced, staring across the table as if they hadn't even been there. He was lost in his own little world.

The door clicked shut, and John murmured, "That guy gives me the creeps."

Adele blinked, holding her eyes closed for a moment longer before opening them again. "I think he's sad. I believe him. I think the knife was for himself."

"Doesn't mean he didn't use it on anyone else."

"Are they running it?"

John nodded. "Pascal is getting them to. We should know if the murder weapon matches."

"I don't think it will," Adele said, quietly.

"He was in the area of the murders. He's traveling alone and can't account for his whereabouts on those nights."

"One of the benefits of being alone."

"Why don't you think it's him?"

Adele considered this question for a moment. Maybe she was empathizing too much. She knew the pain of regret, of losing a family member. She knew how it ate at her whether or not she'd been directly to blame. But also... she'd glimpsed something in the beleaguered suspect. She murmured, "He didn't spend a second in there trying to defend himself. He wasn't angry at us. He just seemed defeated. Why would a man on the verge of suicide, filled with that much guilt, want to go hunt others?"

"He's killed before," John said.

Adele rubbed at her eyes, feeling the lack of sleep slowly catching up with her. "He was charged, but not convicted," she said. "It was deemed an accident."

"Doesn't mean it was. This guy was on the pilgrimage. He said so himself. He matches the description. He has a sketchy past."

"We can send his picture to the landlady—see if she recognizes him."

John frowned at this, scratching his chin. "You don't think she will?"

"No. I don't. And if it's not him, where does that leave us?"

"But what if it is?"

"The knife doesn't even match the murder weapon, John. The coroners all said the same thing. The murder weapon wasn't a knife. Their throats were cut, but with something else."

"So what do you think we should do? Clearly you want to get moving again, yes?"

"We can wait for Pascal to show the photo. If the landlady IDs him, problem solved."

John shook his head. "I hate it when you say it like that. You're not convinced."

Adele glanced at her partner. "Are you?"

He sighed, and then shook his head once. "I guess not. Fine, I'll talk to Pascal. We'll see if anything else shows up. In the meantime, though, if he isn't our guy, you'll have a hell of a time convincing the Spanish authorities of that. They're getting pressure to clear the pilgrimage routes—people are upset they're being watched by police while they conduct their sacred journey."

"We'll be done when we're done. They might not like it, but I can think of at least three people who would've been glad for us to show up on time." Adele leaned back against the metal interrogation room door and gave another long sigh. The world weighed in, and it felt heavy. Her shoulders ached under the pressure, along with her thoughts. Mr. Segura seemed racked with guilt, filled with self-loathing. Could it have led him to kill? He didn't even have the energy to defend himself. He'd been eating supper when they'd arrived, and it had taken everything in him just to get to his feet. Would he really be able to summon the energy to outmatch someone like Matthew? Or Rosa? Would he have killed Father Fernando? She didn't think so. She knew hunches could be wrong but the murder weapon didn't match either.

What was the killer using? Calcium carbonate. Not a bone, surely? Something of religious significance?

Adele pushed off the door, growling as she did and moving down the hall in the direction of the conference room where Agent Pascal was still arguing with the precinct's sergeant on duty.

They needed answers. And they needed them now.

CHAPTER TWENTY FIVE

He could feel his heart pounding as he hopped the fence, wincing against the pain along his side. His hands were still scraped and bloody from the close call with the truck, and now...

Now he had stooped so low to *steal*.

The bike in his hands was old, rusted—no gears, even. He'd ignored a few other, far nicer bikes in order to snatch one that someone might not miss.

But it was still theft.

He'd told a lie to the woman at the hostel, giving a false name. And now he'd stolen a bike.

He could feel his heart hammering as he settled on the seat, adjusted his cotton handkerchief to the handlebars, and began to pedal, picking up speed, faster, faster. He pedaled until his legs ached again, ignoring the fire in his right side. Was his ankle badly sprained?

Perhaps, but it didn't matter. Pain would purify. It always had.

His mind darted back... more memories. Memories he'd cherished. *"Evil creature! On the ground, worm! On the ground."* The flash of pain across his shoulders. The whistle of the metal buckle on the end of the belt as it struck him again and again. *"On the ground!"*

He winced, pedaling faster, ignoring the pain in his ankle, teeth set, eyes ahead. He couldn't slow, couldn't stop now. He had to keep going, going.

He'd lied. He'd stolen.

But absolution awaited. Absolution for all his sins. Absolution for everything. He just needed to reach the cathedral. He pedaled, his heart pounding as he raced to the top of a hill and began to coast down now. Still, even then, he pedaled. Without gears, it was difficult to manage the speed, but he'd faced greater obstacles.

Sleep and exhaustion from the day's travels were falling on him now, but he couldn't stop. Now wasn't the time to slow. He had to press on.

Faster. Faster

Further.

He had to ride hard to make up for lost time. He couldn't stop tonight. Sleep was for the weak. Food was for the gluttons. Pain only deterred the pleasure-craving. No… he could make it. He would make it.

He continued to pedal, his legs aching, his body on fire, his head down, gasping in quiet breaths and tearing through the night under the watchful eye of the stars and moon.

He had to reach the cathedral. He needed to reach the shrine.

***

Adele stood outside the precinct as night returned to make itself known. A day wasted. A day of interrogation, of broken promises. She still didn't know what to make of John. Renee had been acting strange—she should have trusted her instincts.

Why hadn't he told her? Not only that—did she want to be with the sort of man who abandoned his daughter? Was it even any of her business?

She clenched her teeth, trying to refocus, to rip away from this line of thinking.

As she stood outside the precinct, eyes half-hooded behind the night sky, she considered the first victim on the case. Father Gabriel Fernando. A priest…

Why did it matter he was a priest?

The religious ties in this case were clear…

So why kill a priest?

If the killer was seeking some sort of absolution, clearly he held the church in high regard. So why kill a man of the cloth?

It didn't sit right. She was missing something.

Something else nagged at her… The name he'd given to the landlady, then apologized for it, saying he'd been lying. None of it made sense. But the name… Just a throwaway name? Or something more?

Adele frowned, slowly pulling her phone out from her pocket and swiping to the internet browser. What were the odds?

What name had he given again? Oh, right…

She typed in the search bar, Ricardo Mora.

She waited as the search engine began to load…

No results, save a few profiles on social media sites.

She cursed, considering a moment longer… Why had he killed Father Fernando? Why had this all started in Saint-Jean-Pied-de-Port?

She typed in "Ricardo Mora," and then, before hitting enter, she also added the commune's name.

She let out a little sigh and hit Search.

Results popped up nearly instantly. This time, not from social media sites, but from local news articles. All of them in Spanish.

She scowled, clicking over to the app the department used to translate web pages. Little more than a glorified browser translation service, it would have to suffice unless she wanted to go fetch Agent Pascal.

For now, this was nothing more than a hunch.

She waited patiently as the page began to translate to French.

As she scanned the translated sections of the article, she wrinkled her nose. A few sentences were complete gibberish, others were missing words or subjects entirely.

But as she scanned the paragraphs, pieces began to fall into place. Feeling her eyes widen, she clicked on another article, also translating this one.

Now, using the combination of the two half-translated pages, she could feel her heartbeat quickening.

Not just a hunch.

A clue.

Ricardo Mora… Or, according to these articles… Father Mora. A priest…

But not just any priest. A priest who, ten years ago, had been in the same commune as Father Gabriel Fernando. The first victim.

The same commune where the first victim had been killed.

Adele could feel her heart racing now, her pulse quickening to catch up with her racing thoughts. Ricardo Mora had died under suspicious circumstances at the same commune. He'd drowned… The first article hadn't been clear, translating a certain word as "rock star."

Really, though, as Adele looked it up manually, the word in question meant "idol." A small stone statue had been found in Mora's pocket where he'd drowned.

Strange. An idol?

Why did that matter?

Perhaps the same way the money found in Rosa Alvarez's pocket mattered. Or the condoms on Father Fernando… And Matthew… He'd been found with an empty sandwich wrapper. Small, strange things. Nothing on their own, especially this last one. But maybe the killer had been rushed.

What did they mean together, though?

Not just clues, but accusations.

Adele stared at the translated page of the longer article. It showed a picture of the commune and the Gothic church she'd visited first. The first crime scene.

Apparently, Father Mora had been at the commune when there'd also been a school on the premises. The school had now turned into an orphanage—hadn't one of the priests mentioned they worked with orphans, teaching classes?

Did it matter?

Why had the killer given a fake name of a dead priest?

She hesitated, considering it for a moment, and then she fished the business card John had given her for Father Paul. She dialed the number, lifting her phone beneath the evening sky. She waited, impatiently, as the phone began to ring.

She took a couple of steps away from the precinct, toward the parking lot, if only to keep her blood flowing. Exhaustion hung heavy on her, caffeine circling her system. She couldn't fall asleep, though. Not yet.

On the third ring, a voice answered.

"Hello?"

"Father Paul?" Adele said.

"I—yes… Ah, Agent Sharp, correct? I recognize your voice."

"Yes, er, sir. Look, I'm calling about something. Did you know a man name Ricardo Mora?"

"I—not personally, no," said the voice on the other end, the tone turning a bit colder than how it had started.

"But you've heard of him?"

"He was before my time, child. I only came here seven years ago."

"I see. I'm… Has anything else happened in your commune in your tenure there, or in recent history?"

"Anything else? Many things happen here, child."

"No, sir—that's not what I mean. Anything… noteworthy?"

"Are you referring to Father Fernando's death?"

"I know about Fernando. I know about Mora's drowning."

"That was a horrible accident."

"So the reports concluded. But anything else—anything I should know about?" Adele felt frustrated, flailing for words that she couldn't quite seize hold of. She wasn't sure exactly *what* she was looking for.

For a moment silence reigned and Adele though perhaps she'd lost reception. But then a long sigh emanated on the other end.

"Ah, I think I know what you're talking about. I can assure you, Agent Sharp, he was one bad apple. The rest of us voted unanimously to bring it to the church at large. No one holds ill will about it. Is that what you're wondering?"

Adele frowned. She paused, considering her reply. She didn't have a clue what Paul was talking about, but also didn't want to lose this small glint of bait. So instead, she said, "What did you think about all of that?"

"Well... It's obviously not great for the reputation of the commune or the church here. Besides, excommunicating a priest is a very rare occurrence. Even in France. None of us wanted it to go that way. But times are changing—protecting each other is a commandment of the Lord. We believe in protecting our brothers and fathers. But we can't do it at the cost of others. It's a tricky balance and I pray for discretion and wisdom daily. At the time, I, along with the others here, felt that Vargas was going well beyond the pale."

"Vargas?" Adele said, frowning.

"Yes. Brother Luca Vargas," Paul replied. "That's who you're asking about, isn't it?"

Adele paused again, collecting her thoughts. "You're telling me you had a priest excommunicated from your church. When?"

"Hang on—what are you asking about?"

"Now? That."

She heard a sigh, and another long pause continued.

"I really shouldn't be—"

"I will come there myself and take you to an interrogation room if you don't," Adele snapped.

The man on the other end sighed again. "Your threats don't affect me, child. Those in my faith have suffered far worse at the hands of jackbooted thugs."

She winced, biting her lip. Quickly, she said, "Apologies. I shouldn't have spoken like that. But this isn't about saving the church's reputation right now. It's related to a murder investigation. Three are dead. Three innocents. That's what you just said, yes? It's important to protect your own, but also not at the sake of others. Well, others are being hurt. I need your help. Please."

Father Paul sighed again, his voice crackling for a moment as if he'd walked through a patch of bad reception. Still crackling, he finally said, "I understand your zeal, Agent Sharp. I don't blame you. I ... I hate speaking ill of a brother. Especially one as sick as Mr. Vargas. He grew up in this commune, in fact. Went to the school here. Started teaching after finishing his studies."

"Luca Vargas. He was a priest?"

"Used to be. No longer. He... he was excommunicated for archaic practices. Punishments like flogging and self-flagellation. He hurt himself, but also encouraged some of his students to hurt themselves. He was caught whipping a fourteen-year-old boy."

Paul drifted off for a moment. When he spoke next, his tone was laden with emotion as if he were on the verge of sobbing. "I—I'd never seen anything like that. It scared me when I heard. I can't imagine the sort of wounding for the boy either. It certainly wasn't the light of the church, nor was it the light of Christ. We let down the people most vulnerable." His voice still strained with emotion. "It hurt me to do it. It hurt all of us. But Mr. Vargas was sick. He wasn't well. He needed help and he couldn't be trusted in his priestly duties. Not everyone is meant to be a priest. The Lord gifts us all in different ways, Agent Sharp. Like you. You're gifted to find people that hurt others."

"And this Mr. Vargas, after he was excommunicated, how did he react?"

Father Paul sighed wearily. "He left. He was angry, of course. He saw his practices as righteous atonement. But it was practically torture. He believed no one was without sin. We agree with this, of course. All have fallen short of the glory of God. But it's with outreached arms, a desire to serve and love and offer mercy, that we approach the hurting and the wounded. With a giant dose of humility, knowing none of us have any right to judge others... There but for the grace of God go I... Do you know this saying?"

"I've heard it before," Adele said quietly, remembering Robert Henry saying those very words to her not long ago in his home office. "Would this Luca Vargas be in our system? Did he get arrested?"

"It wasn't taken that far," Father Paul replied. "The child he whipped refused to press charges. Eventually, after he was excommunicated, it was dropped."

"Do you happen to have a photo of Luca Vargas?"

"I can send one. Yes. We have our own files. It will take me a bit to get to the library. Maybe half an hour."

Adele was already stalking toward their borrowed police car, frowning as she moved. "Can you make it fifteen? I'm in a hurry."

"I can try, child. Be safe, Agent Sharp. I'll send you his photo when I can. Please—please consider, Mr. Vargas is not well. Whatever harm he's caused, I assure you he's suffered too."

"Thanks for the advice, Paul. Please, send me that photo. Quickly."

Adele hung up, throwing open the front door to the waiting vehicle and sliding into the seat, already jamming the keys into the ignition.

Luca Vargas.

That was their killer. She knew it as deep as her bones.

Now she just had to find him.

Thankfully, she knew exactly where he was going.

CHAPTER TWENTY SIX

His breath came in broken gasps, his eyes stinging from the sweat and blood intermingling and pouring down his face. The scrape marks from where his cheek had rubbed off on the road now also stung with the evidence of his exertion.

He wheeled the no-gear bike along at his side, puffing and limping. Ahead, as he looked up, he thought he spotted the outline of some structure against the night. He narrowed his eyes, staring in the direction of the protrusion. The many jutting spires stood out like fingers against the sky. He went still for a moment. His legs felt like fire, his eyes and cuts in pain. The throbbing sensation from his ankle up his thigh had worsened.

And yet, as he stared at the structure in the distance, he felt like a man in the desert stumbling on an oasis.

The cathedral. He'd arrived in Santiago de Compostela.

A soft sob escaped his lips. Tears formed in his eyes despite his dehydration. His hand lifted from the handlebars of the bike, allowing the cotton handkerchief to flutter as it fell along with the bicycle toward the ground.

One shouldn't litter.

He knew this.

And yet he was so close now.

Absolution wasn't just a matter of the conscience, it was one of the soul.

He let out a whimpering little sigh, taking a tottering step forward on weak legs, moving down the dusty path. His back ached, his body ached, but his eyes—stinging still—were glued to the front steps of the incredible Santiago de Compostela Cathedral. The thing seemed to have been taken from the days long past. A magnificent structure, an architectural wonder of its time, with sky-high turrets and spires and a beige, multi-faceted facade. A thing of beauty and awe. An imposing, powerful structure. He could feel the power even now, emanating from within. St. James had been buried here—at least that's what the rumors held. Though he didn't consider them rumors—he knew they were true. How could they not be?

He'd come this far—come so long. Even in the dark, against the night, the beauty of the magnificent architectural achievement beckoned him closer. Both ancient but rigid, worn but strong.

He sobbed then stepped, sobbed then stepped. His ankle didn't just feel sprained—perhaps it was even broken. All his time as a priest, once upon a time, in another life, had given him knowledge of many things. Including, at times, first aid. It helped him now how to properly break down a body. Often his own. The Lord supplied the knowledge he'd needed.

Once upon a time, he'd been confronted by another priest from his old church in the old commune. But the man hadn't understood, had he? A narrow-focused man, throwing accusations about...

He sobbed, his shoulders heavy under the weight of sin, of guilt...

Ten years he'd carried the burden. Ten years he'd carried what he'd done.

Father Mora hadn't deserved it. Father Mora had been the only righteous one among them. Hadn't he shown it? Hadn't he brought pain as a gift?

Now, limping toward his final destination, Luca Vargas could feel his heart quicken. He remembered all the times Father Mora had scourged him, beaten him. All the times he'd been bloodied and bruised. Penitence, atonement... These things were crucial.

He limped again, hissing beneath his breath.

Father Mora had been a mistake...

The man had carried a little statue. Idolatry—or a younger Luca had thought so, at least. He hadn't meant to drown the man. Hadn't meant to kill the only father he'd ever known.

No parents of his own, no family, no friends to speak of. Father Mora had taken him in, sheltered him, taught him pain. He'd gone to the school, fortunate enough to be allowed in by Mora. The same man who'd beaten him, who'd dragged him from his bunk in the night to whip him. Mora had been a harsh man, a tasking father—but one who'd made Luca into the person he was today. He would've remained weak, pathetic, full of sin and self-loathing if not for Father Mora's ministrations.

And how had he repaid the man?

He'd drowned him.

Not on purpose. He'd thought the Lord had given him a sign. But the priest hadn't been engaged in idolatry. He'd simply been confiscating a statue from one of the students. The truth had come out later.

Luca whimpered, taking another step, dragging his right foot behind him now. It was going numb from the pain—he could barely feel it. One step. Another. Another. He focused on the ground, creating imaginary lines in his mind. Just two more steps.

He did it.

Now just two more.

Again he did it.

Just two more.

Like this, he traveled a few hundred feet up the old road under the watchful night.

Father Mora had taught him to be attentive, taught him to keep an eye out for sin. Luca had thought he'd been obedient, even calling Mora out. They'd struggled. The old man had fallen into the well. Luca had thought it a judgment of God, but then he realized his mistake.

He whimpered at the memories, at the desperate cry from the old man as he'd plummeted into the well.

After that, things had only gotten worse. He'd increased the punishments on himself, on the students under him. The only way toward purity was pain. He increased his efforts out of contrition, out of repentance. By doing what Father Mora had done, he thought perhaps he could absolve himself. But he should have known better. He'd killed a good man. Taken a life without permission… And so he had paid the due penalty in his flesh for the hardening of his own heart.

The guilt of what he'd done had eaten at him, nearly consuming him.

He let out a shattered breath, finally reaching the bottom step to the cathedral. So close… so very close.

He stared at the open door of the structure. The burial place of St. James. It all lay before him. Ten long years. Ten years of waiting for the Lord's permission.

He'd gone through a Job season. Found himself like Jonah in the belly of the whale.

He whimpered, another step, onto the bottom stair now. So smooth, so welcoming. At night, no one watched. A few people further down the road were heading in the other direction. He was alone now, taking the steps toward his destiny.

For a decade he'd suffered. Three years after his horrible sin, he'd been excommunicated. After that, he'd fallen into penance. As he'd continued, he'd felt the call of God louder in his mind, whispering at first, but growing. As a child, he'd enjoyed hurting others. One of the reasons Mora had been so hard on him. Now, of course, he didn't enjoy it… At least, he would never admit it. Not that there was anything left to admit. He simply fulfilled the Lord's judgment. Pain... Pain only gave him pleasure because it was how it had to be. A sort of spiritual hedonism.

He knew his path to absolution would require judgment of others.

Three souls he'd already offered. Three unrepentant sinners.

None of them would have made this journey. Not like he had.

"I am here, Lord," he said, smiling now at the sky, looking toward the clouds reflecting the moon. "I have come... You called and I answered. I am just a humble servant."

He outstretched his hands for a moment, standing in the middle of the stairs, inhaling in, out, deeper, louder, filling his lungs with air.

The final breaths of a sinful man. The final breaths of a soul unfulfilled. Now... steps away, everything would change. Like the Apostle Paul often said, in the twinkling of an eye, this great mystery, he would become in the likeness of the lamb.

Just a twinkle. A flash of achievement.

So very close.

He swallowed, licking his parched lips, his eyes too dry to tear up now, his body too dehydrated to sweat.

As he moved up the final few steps toward the entrance into the ancient cathedral, a voice suddenly called from the shadows behind a pillar.

"Stop," the voice said, simply.

He hesitated, frowning.

"Lord?" he murmured.

"No," the voice replied. "Not your God. DGSI. Don't move, Luca Vargas. Keep your hands where I can see them."

He turned, frowning, as a woman stepped from behind the incredible tan, contoured columns, and moved in front of the shadowy door, only paces away from him. She stood at the top of the stairs, glaring down at him, her chin jutting out in defiance, her hands at her side. One hand rested on a firearm.

He stared, swallowing. "You know my name?"

She scowled at him, nodding once. "Yes, Luca. I know where you've been. I know what you've done. Stop where you are."

He whimpered now, staring over her shoulder into the cathedral. The door was so large around her, swallowing the woman's slight frame. She was taller than most—only barely shorter than him. She had long blonde hair, pulled back, and her face was like granite, fixed in a foreboding expression.

"I—I can speak in a moment, child," he said softly. "I must first enter this place."

She crossed her arms, though, fixating him with an unyielding expression. "No. That's not going to happen. You're not going in."

He blinked, stunned, and looked at her, his mouth forming a small circle. "I—excuse me?"

"You're not going in," she said, firmly, shaking her head. "Keep your hands up—or this is going to go poorly for you."

He began to raise his hands slowly. His expression fluttered, the pain along his side flaring again. What did she mean he wasn't allowed in?

"Who—who are you?" he whispered.

"My name is Agent Sharp. I work with the DGSI and Interpol. And I'm telling you, I won't let you in."

"You can't stop me!" he said, scandalized and stunned more than angry. "Please—please!" His voice became a screech and he raised his extended hands imploringly in her direction. "Please—you have to let me in. You have to!" His voice became a howl now.

But the woman in the doorway didn't budge. He tried to limp forward, but her gun pulled from her holster. She kept it facing the stairs between them. But the threat was obvious. "Not another step," she snapped.

He licked his lips, judging the distance between them. Maybe if he could get a hand over the doorway—even the edge of his pinky... perhaps that would be enough. He stared into the doorway, stared past the woman as if she wasn't even there. The darkness called to him, invited him. The night around them cradled him, comforting him.

Hadn't it been night when Mora had fallen into the well? Fallen— yes... he'd fallen, hadn't he? Just a sad accident. Of course... Just an accident.

He had never intended to hurt anyone. It wasn't his fault. The Lord told him.

"I don't enjoy it," he said, breathlessly, louder now. "I—I don't. I swear."

"You swear?" the woman said, shaking her head. "I thought you weren't supposed to swear."

"I—it... Let me through!" he snarled, taking a lunging step forward.

But the gun snapped up, pointing toward his chest.

"Get back, now!" she snarled. "I will drop you where you stand."

CHAPTER TWENTY SEVEN

Adele stood with her feet shoulder width, gun raised, fixed on the man three steps lower. He looked in a bad way, as if he'd been in a fight or an accident. Blood trickled down the side of his face, scrape marks that hadn't been bandaged in hours, by the looks of them. His leg dragged with his motion, suggesting he was limping. His eyes were bloodshot, wide. His hair was half combed to the side, held by gel, but the other half was disheveled and wild, jutting every which way. In one hand, he gripped at his pocket, holding onto something she couldn't see, hidden in the folds of his fabric.

She stared at Luca Vargas, stared at the excommunicated priest. The church had gotten it right this time. They'd kicked this man from their ranks. She wondered if they'd known just how good of a call that had been.

Now this fellow stood before her, one hand groping at his pocket, his lips parted as a soft, whimpering mewl echoed into the night. His eyes darted about wildly, shooting looks of longing through the doorway behind her.

To Adele, it was just an old cathedral. She understood the history, the culture, the faith. She respected it. But she didn't believe walking a few hundred miles would save someone from their past. She'd experienced too much pain to think any human effort could do that.

But to this man…

What lay behind her was absolution.

Was a way to rewind time.

A way to erase his memory.

"Rosa Alvarez," she murmured. "Gabriel Fernando," she said, louder. "Matthew Icardi."

He blinked, shaking his head. "I—please…"

He tried to step forward again, but again she pointed her gun at him, snapping, "Don't!"

"Please," he whimpered again, mewling like a kitten without milk. His hand at his side kept twisting and turning in his pocket, tracing the counters of some item hidden in the fabric.

"Why did you kill them?" she said, slowly. "What did they do to you?"

He stared at her. "Killed?"

"Yes—you wouldn't lie to me, would you? Like you lied to the lady back at the hostel. You lied about your name, Mr. Vargas."

"Father Vargas!" he snapped, looking at her for the first time as if just realizing who she was. "Father Vargas, child!"

The man had dark hair tinged with gray and his face was streaked with lines of age and worry. He looked as if he might be in his forties, but around his eyes he looked sixty.

"You were excommunicated, weren't you?" Adele said softly. "For violence against those in your charge."

"I didn't mean to lie to that lady," he said. "I apologized. I told her the truth."

"You did—didn't you. That's important to you, hmm?" Adele said, carefully, her eyes flicking along the man's countenance, trying to read an indeterminable page. "Truth is important."

"It is."

"So why did you kill them?"

"Who?"

"Rosa Alvarez," Adele said, through gritted teeth, speaking more firmly. "Matthew Icardi. Gabriel Fernando."

"I don't know those names... I—wait, yes, Matthew. The glutton? Hmm? I think I know the name Matthew. The others I don't know."

Adele stared at him. "You don't even know their names?"

"The sinners?" he said, surprised all of a sudden. "Are you asking about the sinners I punished?"

She wet her lips, swallowing slowly. "Yes. Yes, them. Why did you kill them?"

"I didn't—the Lord did. I was just his vessel, see," he said quickly, his tone relieved now as if certain this explanation would clear everything up. He gave a good-natured chuckle. "Dear Lord, you had me worried there for a moment. I'm afraid you're mistaken. Here, just let me step past you and we can discuss whatever you'd like, child."

"I'm not your child. You're not a priest. You killed them. Why?"

His jaw set and Adele could tell he was growing angry. "The glutton? The whore? The homosexual?" He waved a hand beneath his chin as if to say, *hurry up.*

"So they hurt you in some way?"

"It's not about harm, child. No-harm morality is a secular invention. I don't believe in no-harm morality. The Lord doesn't." He jammed a finger at the night sky. "No-harm means nothing. Sin always harms. Eventually. Even over time. Sometimes hundreds of years later. If you could trace the path of a lie, a theft, a broken promise—if you could trace the effect through the centuries, you would turn paradise to hell. There is no harmless sin. None!"

"What about murder? Is that a sin?"

"Judgment!" he crowed, arms spreading wide again. "Not murder! Not murder!" His one hand went back to his pocket, twisting furiously. "I didn't *murder* anyone. Is it not the Lord's will to judge? I simply fulfilled his commands."

"You're not God. You don't get to kill people because you enjoy it."

He spat. "I don't enjoy it! I never have. Never!"

"I think you're lying to yourself." Adele could feel the way her gun went cold in her fingers. The way the steel pressed against her hand. She could feel the wind ushering up the steps, over the killer's shoulders, ruffling her hair.

She also could feel the certainty in her bones.

She wouldn't move. She wasn't going to allow him into the cathedral.

She thought of her mother, of Robert Henry. She thought of the small monster with the dull eye and the limp. She thought of the tortures he'd inflicted, of the horrors he'd wrought. Of the way he'd taunted her, stalked her, taken a shot at her father. The way he'd nearly killed John once. She thought of how systematically he'd gone out of his way to dismantle every moment of joy and beauty in her life.

A man like that didn't deserve absolution.

She was sure a theologian could argue with her, could tell her the wrong way of her thinking. Didn't everyone need forgiveness? Didn't every sinner need saving?

She'd heard it all before.

And she didn't care.

This man wasn't going to pass her. He couldn't murder and get away with it. That wasn't how life worked. He was trying to pass her to clear his conscience, that was all. But he didn't deserve a clear conscience. He didn't even remember the names of the people he'd brutally slain. They were nothing to him. If anything, he seemed proud of what he'd done. He was now watching her as if she were little more than an annoying gnat. If he could, no doubt he would have tried to crush her for the simple crime of intervening in his own desires.

He killed because he wanted to. She knew killers, she could sniff it on them.

This was a murderer. He couched it in holier-than-thou language, he hid among sheep as a wolf, but it didn't change what he was. It didn't

141

change the glaring hated behind his eyes.

"You started with Ricardo Mora, didn't you? Why? Ten years ago. They said he drowned by accident. But you were there at the time. Did you do it?"

It was as if she'd struck him across the face. He gasped, staring up at her, mouth unhinged, his face turning suddenly pale as if he'd seen a ghost.

"What did you say to me?" he murmured.

"Ricardo Mora," she repeated. "Say his name. Say it with me. Say, *I killed Ricardo Mora*. Say it! Say it!" She was yelling now, her own anger rising within her, images of her mother's corpse, of Robert's... The way they'd been mutilated, choking on their own blood, tortured for hours. The killer had teased her once—the way they'd screamed. He'd laughed about it. He'd enjoyed it, and he'd wanted her to know that her mother's pain, her surrogate father's pain, had given him pleasure. Not for any other reason but because he enjoyed the agony it caused her.

"Say it," she growled, her finger trembling against the trigger. "Say his name. Robert Henry. Say it! Say it, dammit!"

"Who?" the man said, still shaking, still pale, his hand still in his pocket. "I don't know Robert Henry. Father Mora was a mistake—a horrible, horrible error. I've repented for it. I have! I flogged myself for years over it. See! See!" he twisted at the waist, lifting up his shirt and displaying a spine crisscrossed with thick, roping scars. His eyes were blazing now, shaking his head. "Do not perform your acts of righteousness before men to be seen by them!" he declared. "I did what I had to. I didn't mean to hurt him. It was a mistake. I misunderstood the Lord."

"You killed a man. Why? Was he hurting you? Is that it? Is that your pathetic excuse for all this—for everything you're doing?"

"Do... hot... perform..." His chest heaved now, his face still white, his lips trembling where he stood on the steps beneath the giant cathedral. Adele could feel the way his eyes kept flicking toward the entrance behind her.

She didn't budge an inch. She refused to. He was delusional—that much was clear. He truly believed the crazed ravings he muttered. He truly believed all of it justified his actions. The taking of three lives. Perhaps even four.

He lowered his other hand now, speaking softer, quieter, an even tone to his voice all of a sudden. "I understand you're angry. I understand you don't see the judgment of God. But child, please, let me explain. They were sinners. The Glutton, the Whore, the Homosexual. They were sinners. They were put in my path for the sake of truth. For the sake of judgment. The Lord did it. I begged him, I really did, I pleaded with the Lord to not make me do it. I asked him to pass the cup... but should I not obey? Is it up to me to decide his will?"

"So that's it, then?" Adele whispered. "You kill sinners? Hmm? Like some sort of cosmic crap shoot. Some he loves. Some he kills. And you get to decide, is that right? I was just speaking to an old friend of yours. Someone from your commune." She was careful not to mention Father Paul's name. "He said the role of priests is to extend mercy. Where was your mercy? Hmm? You don't like sinners. Well, I'm a sinner. What are you going to do about it?" She wasn't even sure what she was saying now. She could feel the adrenaline bruiting through her system, could feel the way her nostrils widened as she inhaled rapidly.

She didn't take it back though. She meant it. "What are you going to do?" she demanded.

"You are a sinner?" he said. "Then you should enter with me." He pointed past her. "Did you complete the pilgrimage? Did you walk the way?"

"You didn't walk," she snapped. "You biked. You can't even play fair at your own game."

"The Lord allows it!" he snapped. "Who are you to judge me?"

"Who are you?" she yelled back. The streets had cleared, night had captured this section of the city. The cathedral was quiet. Only the janitors, some security remained, but they were further in. No one came to investigate the raised voices. No one even seemed to notice.

"I sin," she said, wagging her head, gun clutched in one hand. "I sin all the time. When I was fifteen, my first swimming coach, he was gorgeous. Absolutely stunning. A six-pack like you wouldn't believe. I can't tell you how many times I lusted after him. I lusted after him poolside. I lusted after him in the shower at home. Sometimes, I still imagine him. I imagine him slipping off those tight swim trunks. I imagine what he has beneath. Hmm? Is that all right? Is that sin enough for you?"

He was staring at her, red-faced now, gaping like a suffocating fish.

"I lie too," she said, emphatically. "I lied to my father just last week about where I'd hidden his beer. I drink also. Lots of times. I've been drunk. What do you think about that? Hmm?"

"Stop it!" he snarled. "Stop talking!"

"Sometimes when I was young I would lust *and* drink. Together.

143

Astonishing, really. Want to know what else? I've also killed. More than once. I've shot men like you dead. I've watched them bleed out." Here, trembling, her finger still shaky on the trigger, she leaned in, her face jutting over her extended weapon. She dropped her voice to a stage whisper, feeling something rising in her chest that made the fury all the more potent. "Want to know something? Something secret? Something I'm never supposed to say?"

"Quiet, whore! Be quiet!"

"Sometimes," she pressed on, even louder than him, "sometimes, I enjoy it when they die. I try to pretend I don't. I want to be a good person. I hate when I feel that way. But sometimes... sometime I like it. I like watching monsters who have killed and murdered and maimed bleed out. I like it when they die. And so, *bitch*," she spat, "I'm not letting you in. I don't give a fucking shit, you ugly piece of wasted life. I am *not* fucking letting you in! So what are you going to do? Huh?" She was yelling now. "What? What are you going to do?"

For a moment, the man just stared at her, stunned, clearly in some sort of shock. She wasn't sure if he'd ever been spoken to like this before. Part of her felt an odd thrill of satisfaction. Another part of her only felt horror at her own words. Did she even realize what she was saying? Her heart hammered wildly. Did she really mean all of that?

She supposed part of her did. At least now. At least in this moment, a part of her meant every word. Another part of her felt only shame she'd said any of it—mostly the last parts. The part about enjoying the death of a suspect. It was true, though.

She knew it was true. She hated that it was true. More often than not, her better nature won out. She had once administered first aid to a serial killer, trying to save him after he'd tried to murder her. She'd saved the life of a rapist before too, protecting him from drowning.

But there had been other times... She didn't shed tears for the monsters of the night.

Should she? Did that make her evil? Maybe she was a sinner after all...

But she'd said her piece, and she'd meant it.

She wasn't going to step aside. Of that, she was certain.

He licked his lips, eyes circling inside their sockets, and then, snuffling and growling, he pulled out the item he'd been fingering in his pocket.

A seashell.

A scallop—Adele recognized it briefly. One of the symbols of St. James—she'd done her research now.

144

"That's what you use," she said, breathlessly, staring at the scallop. "You killed them with a fucking seashell."

"Stop swearing. Stop it, whore!"

She stared at the scallop, and then, eyes hooded, she looked the killer dead in the face. "Or what?"

Finally, he seemed to lose it. He snarled, screaming at the sky, and then he lunged at her, ducking low under the line of fire and whipping his scallop toward her hand.

CHAPTER TWENTY EIGHT

Luca Vargas lunged at Adele, and she felt her finger tighten on the trigger.

In a brief moment, she knew she had a clear shot. She could have taken it. But another, smaller part of her rejected this. She'd goaded him, hadn't she? He wouldn't have attacked if she hadn't said all those things. If she killed him... what did that make her?

She hesitated a second too long, finger on the trigger, but not tightening. In that moment, he managed to shove her gun to the side and surge toward her, shoulder first.

She yelled in pain as his body caught her chest like a battering ram, sending her skidding back on the top step. Something slashed across her throat, and she yelled. For a moment, standing in the shadow of the cathedral entrance, she reached up with trembling fingers, trying to collect herself, to aim once more. Her fingers came away with blood.

He'd cut her. Not too deep, but he'd cut her all the same.

Adele breathed, staring at where her fingers held droplets of red. At the same time, her eyes refocused on the man at the top step. He came charging at her, trying to lurch past her into the cathedral. But she wouldn't let him. She lunged forward as well. Again, if she'd waited, she could've had a clear shot. But also, if she'd waited, it would have allowed him into the cathedral. This wasn't an option. So instead, she barreled into him, sending her shoulder into his chest, returning the favor. The man howled, stumbling back, tripping and cursing as his leg bent under him. His right side was weak. Something had hurt him. Now, gasping, he tried to regain his feet, pushing up on one knee. His scallop had fallen on the ground, resting on the marble floor between them.

Adele's eyes narrowed. She stepped forward and slammed her foot down. A piece of evidence—she knew she shouldn't have done it. In that moment, though, she wasn't acting as an FBI agent. *This* was what he'd used to kill—this thing was precious to him. So she smashed it. The scallop crushed into a dozen pieces. She kicked them, sending them scattering.

For a moment, one hand on the ground, trying to regain his balance, Luca just stared at what she'd done. He gaped, shaking, and then burst into a rage. His face went red, his eyes bloodshot. He screamed incoherently and dove at her. This time, he knocked her gun to the side. Her weapon went scattering into the cathedral itself. Instead of lunging after it, though, she dragged her fingers across the man's face, scraping flash, gripping the collar of his shirt and dragging him back away from the door. Again, he seemed to try to ignore her, stepping past her to reach the cathedral and again, she refused to let him. He yelped, shouting, "Let me go. Lord help me. Let me go."

But she held on for dear life. He kicked back at her, once, twice. Her lip exploded, blood pooled into her mouth with a salty tang.

But still she held on. He managed to scramble over her, crushing her forearm against the marble step. He tried to crawl on his knees, surging toward the door. But she, gasping, got on top of him. Pulling herself onto him, sitting on his back and holding him down so he couldn't reach the cathedral.

He extended his hand, fingers scrambling toward the shadow of the archway. But she grabbed this too, yanking him back and shoving him. Again, he slipped down the top two steps. And again he let out a horrible scream. Gasping, growling, he pulled himself to his full height. He was bleeding from his face, limping horribly, and now had slash marks across his throat from where she'd dragged her fingernails. Adele glanced over her shoulder, into the cathedral. Her gun was lying on the tiles. She could see it just within. She also knew if she went for it, the killer would have ample time to enter after her.

Certainly this wasn't by the book. She could only imagine what Agent Renee would think when he found out. But she wasn't going for her gun. She refused to let him enter. So she stood, arms raised, waiting in the threshold of the cathedral, glaring. The killer was disarmed, his seashell shattered. Her gun was behind her. The two of them glared at each other, both of them injured, both of them bleeding. Adele spotted a drop of red from her hand spatter toward the ground. Luca stared at this and screamed, "Desecration!" and lunged.

She waited for him to reach her and then kicked, hard, catching him in the gut and sending him doubled over. Wheezing, he tried to grab her throat. Fingers pressed against her neck, but she pushed him back once more. Gasping at the ground, half dead already, he tried to stay on his feet. His leg wasn't responding, though. His right ankle looked in a bad way, bent and crooked off to the side. His face twisted in agony every time he stepped on it. Now, breathing heavily, he let out a horrible shout and tried to charge again. And again, she refused to give him passage.

This time, though, he saw her kick coming. He avoided it, throwing himself onto his busted ankle. He screamed in agony. Adele hadn't thought he would favor that ankle. This was a man who didn't mind pain. He avoided her enough to shove past her. He sent her stumbling to the side, and then, bleeding, gasping, with desperate shouts, he dragged himself up the top step. He crawled, pulling himself toward the open cathedral door. His fingers were a foot away. Half a foot. A few inches. She snarled, lunged, grabbing his ankle with both hands and pulling until it felt like her arms might yank from their sockets. The man howled in horror as he was dragged back once more.

"No!" she snapped. "No," she said, louder, repeating the word. "That's not for you. It's not."

She was breathing heavily, gasping the words like some sort of mantra or battle cry, trying to keep herself focused.

The killer was sobbing now, trying to kick on his floppy right leg. But his ankle was causing him more pain than it did her. She gripped this ankle, holding tight. For a moment she wanted to twist. Just to cause more pain.

But then she realized what she was thinking. Horror welled up in her. She swallowed, shaking, and moved her hands to his other ankle, leaving the injured one. She couldn't. She simply couldn't. If she did, maybe he was right about them. About all of them. Humans. Maybe he was right.

She held his uninjured ankle, holding him in place—and pulled her cuffs out.

The fight seemed to have fled him now, as he was sobbing and bleeding and sweating on the stairs. One hand still stretched, desperately, only a foot away from the entrance to the cathedral. He was crying like a baby, pleading for his mother.

She cuffed him, not too gently. But she was careful to avoid hurting his bad ankle. The man shook, pleading with her. "Please," he said. "Please, let me in. Just a step. That's all. Please. Do what you want with me. But just let me in."

Adele hesitated. She could feel an icy sensation in her stomach, twisting. Could feel the cold fury.

She paused, let out a long sigh, and said, quietly, "What were their names?"

"What?"

"Their names. The ones you killed. What were their names?" She spoke softly now, tired all of a sudden; she just stared down at where his hands were now cuffed behind him. He twisted, whimpering, and staring up at her. "Please, please," he said, desperately.

She wondered if his victims had pleaded. She wondered how it had felt for him to ignore them. He saw them as sinners. He'd seen them as evil. And so he had treated them without mercy. He brutalized them

But *he* was truly evil. She saw him in the way he had seen the others. He didn't even remember their names.

"Please," he said, sobbing again. "I'm begging you. Just a pinky. Just a toe. Just let me in just for a second. I'll do whatever you want. Please."

His shirt had pulled up in the back. She could still see the tapestry of scars all over his body. Had he administered all of these? Had someone else helped?

Her gun was still lying on the tiles in the cathedral.

She glanced at him, glanced toward the door. She leaned in, whispering in his ear, "Rosa Alvarez. Matthew Icardi. Gabriel Fernando. You had *no* right."

He was crying now. Not for the victims. Not for anyone but himself. He didn't care. He had done what he done because he wanted to.

She let out a long sigh, standing on the top steps. John was nowhere nearby. Normally, this was the time he would come in, rushing to the rescue. But she hadn't told him where she was going. She hadn't told anyone. It was as if she'd been working something out for herself. As she stared at the bloody mass of Luca Vargas, she only felt sad. She said, "I have to get my gun. You do what you have to. If you run, you're not going to get far on that ankle. I'll have an ambulance here in a few minutes. They can take care of you."

She didn't feel a single one of those words. All she felt was anger. But it didn't really matter what she felt. The feelings would go and come and go again. What mattered was something else. But she wasn't a theologian. She wasn't a priest. She wasn't a philosopher. She just got bad guys.

Sighing again, she moved through the cathedral's entrance, over toward where her gun was lying on the flagstones. She picked it up, slowly, pushing it into her holster. She waited a few moments, looking around, staring up. It was so dark, night so thick, she could barely make out so much as an archway. It felt fitting, this… She couldn't see the beauty. Couldn't see the splendor. It was just dark.

She let out a long breath, staring into the cathedral. She didn't want to look back. She could hear *him* moving. Could even hear the soft, whimpering sigh of gratitude. She didn't want to see. She couldn't

149

watch. It wasn't up to her if he crawled across the threshold or not. If that was all it took to absolve someone, if that was what it took to make it right, Adele wasn't sure that any of this mattered anyway. She turned back around after another few moments. She waited long enough so she wouldn't have to see. He was still on the top steps, but he looked relieved now, sighing, no longer sobbing. His eyes were closed, his head resting against the top marble step. Had he crawled across? Had he then pulled back? Had he given up?

She wasn't sure. She was glad she didn't know. She stepped back out of the cathedral, gun back in her holster, and stooped, dropping to the steps next to Luca Vargas. His hands were cuffed behind him, and she sat, carefully avoiding blood on one of the steps. Was it hers, his?

She pulled her phone out, calling the paramedics. She sat facing the same direction as Luca. His eyes were still closed. It was as if he was dead, motionless.

She sat on the same step as him, not higher, not lower. She just stared out. She didn't want to hurt him. That wouldn't change anything. She was so sick of it. So sick of them all. People who did this. Who justified what they did. If they could make a monster out of the people they hated, it made violence so much easier. Sometimes there really *were* monsters, though.

Adele held her head in her hands, phone against her cheek as she mumbled into the receiver, but her heart wasn't in it.

The world really had monsters. But that didn't mean she had to enjoy it when they were hurt. That didn't mean her life had to be defined by what they did and how she reacted.

She stared out across the city, sitting on a marble step next to the killer. Her shoulders began to shake. Tears leaked from her eyes, down her cheeks. It wasn't fair.

None of it was fair.

She couldn't make it right. John couldn't make it right. The DGSI couldn't make it right.

She glanced over her shoulder toward the cathedral, staring into the darkness. It seemed so empty. She looked away, tears now falling from her chin and tapping against the bloody steps. She closed her eyes, waiting, sitting next to Luca Vargas and listening for the sounds of approaching sirens.

CHAPTER TWENTY NINE

Adele hadn't slept the night. Almost two days had passed with less than three hours of sleep. She could feel the exhaustion weighing heavy on her. But now, standing outside the precinct, she watched as Mr. Segura took the steps slowly, two at a time, rubbing his wrists.

She watched as he paused at the bottom step and looked up at her. "Thank you," he said, softly.

She nodded once, looking past him across the parking lot. "You gave me your word," Adele said, looking back again. "You're going to finish the pilgrimage."

He swallowed, hesitating for a moment. His emotions were still buried deep. He still didn't seem to react to the same cues one might normally expect in conversational conditioning. But at last, he said, "I'll finish the pilgrimage."

Adele stared at him. Had he killed his brother-in-law? Had it really been an accident? Either way, he knew the victim's name. She could see the horror, the grief in his eyes. That wouldn't change what he had done. But she just didn't have it in her to play judge anymore. He'd been acquitted. And now, he'd said he would finish the pilgrimage. He had threatened to kill himself. But after a night of observation he had been cleared medically. He would finish the pilgrimage. Afterwards, he could do what he wanted. Adele couldn't save everyone. She turned away as the man began to walk, heading toward the street, strolling slowly, hands in his pockets.

Adele's phone began to ring, and she frowned, pulling out the device. Thankfully, it wasn't Agent Paige. "Hello?"

"Agent Sharp?"

"Father Paul."

"Yes, yes, it's me. I apologize for calling you so early." The man cleared his throat on the other end. "I hope I didn't wake you."

Adele sighed, rubbing at her eyes. "No, you didn't. Part of me wish you had. How can I help you, Father?"

The man cleared his throat again uncomfortably. Then, like a tide suddenly being released, he hastily said, "Did you find Vargas? Was it him?"

Adele didn't have the energy to deny it. She just said, "Why are you asking?"

"I just, I felt it was important. I don't think I told you everything."

Adele frowned. "Go on."

"Vargas, he was troubled. We all knew it. We tried to be kind to him. He used to go to the reform school when he was young. It's now an orphanage. The school portion was shut down. I don't like speaking ill of the dead, but that priest you mentioned. The one who died ten years ago..."

"Father Mora?"

"Ricardo, yes. I knew him. Not well. But he had a reputation. I only found out about it afterwards, but there were rumors. Things the church swept under the rug." Father Paul's voice strained again with emotion. The same way it had the night before.

"What sort of rumors?"

"Abuse. A very familiar, sordid story, I'm afraid. Much to our shame. The church has gotten better. Though that's no excuse. Still, all we can do is better. But from the stories I've heard, it was a poorly kept secret that Mora took out some of his more violent tendencies on Vargas and some of the other kids. Many of them had the good sense to get away when they could, but Vargas seemed affectionate of Mora. Like I said, I don't like speaking ill of the dead."

"Why are you telling me this?"

"I want you to know why. If Vargas did this. I want you to know it didn't start with him."

"It didn't have to continue. What's your point?"

Father Paul swallowed. "I don't know if I have a point. But for Vargas, there's every chance that what he did he thought was normal. It was what he was taught from a very young age."

"Everyone has pain," Adele snapped. "It doesn't excuse murder."

"Of course not. I'm not saying that. Just, just don't judge him too harshly."

For a moment, Adele felt like hanging up. She wasn't even sure why. "I don't plan on judging anyone," she said after a moment. "I just catch them. Someone else can decide what happens to them."

"I understand. And Agent Sharp." He hesitated, but then, his voice growing in strength, he said, "I'm very grateful for what you do. You deserve all the credit. Thank you."

She frowned, hesitant. What did he mean? It took her a moment, trying to consider what angle he might be playing, but then she just shrugged. "Thank you. I do what I can. I appreciate the call, Father. Have a good day."

152

"You as well."

"Who was that?" a voice said behind her. She turned, slowly, wearily. Agent John Renee was standing in the sliding doors of the precinct; he hesitated, but then with slow steps he approached.

She looked off across the parking lot again.

"You're asking me who *I'm* calling?" she said, her voice bitter.

"I didn't mean it like that. Look, I was thinking about it. I'm sorry, Adele."

She hesitated, looking back at him. If anything, she hadn't been expecting an apology from Renee. If stubborn had a picture, it would've been a snapshot of John's eyes. Now, though, he was scratching at his scar, glancing toward his feet. He sighed, his large chest rising and falling. "I'm sorry for keeping her secret. I have a daughter—there, I said it. I should've told you. I've not been with anyone for longer than a couple of weeks in more than a decade."

Adele leaned in, too tired to care what social etiquette dictated in this moment. She rested her head against John's chest. For a moment he flinched, but then, instead of pulling away, he pulled her close, putting a large arm around her shoulders and holding her against him. The two of them stared off across the gray parking lot, peering over the vehicles illuminated by the sunlight.

"Thanks for telling me," she said.

"I need to be honest with you, Adele, and that means completely honest."

She didn't have the energy to flinch, but she braced herself.

"I don't want you to meet her. At least not yet. At least not until I get to know her a bit better. I've been thinking about it. Thinking about your father and you. I never saw myself as a father figure. I didn't even have the chance for the first few years of her life. Bernadette didn't want anything to do with me. Not that I blame her. I figured the girl would be better off without me."

Adele relaxed a bit. "I don't need to meet her. I just wanted to know. I care about you. I care about the things that matter to you. I care about the things that *should* matter to you."

She could feel the warmth of John's chest, could practically hear the pounding of his heart. He sighed and gave her shoulder a quick squeeze. "I'll try to be more honest in the future. I—I once had a threesome when I was seventeen—"

Adele winced. "Hang on. You don't have to be *that* honest. Just, you know, the big things. Not every time you had sex. I don't want to know that."

John snorted, but she could tell he was smiling now.

Adele shook her head, still keeping it rested against John's chest. She could forgive him. She knew that. It would take some time, and she hadn't liked that he'd lied about the phone calls. Trust would take a little bit of effort to rebuild. But it would work. She could forgive him.

They stood like that, not looking at anything in particular. There was no sunrise, no beautiful lake, no gorgeous vista. It wasn't like the movies, with swelling music or twittering birds above. There were no symbolic paintings in the background, or moments of self-reflection. It was just the two of them, on the steps of the Spanish precinct, facing a well-maintained parking lot. And it was enough.

Adele found her eyes drooping and for a moment she thought she might fall asleep, leaning as she was.

"John," she said, quietly, "I don't think I'm a good person."

John bristled, tensing. She looked up at him and realized he was scowling. "That's complete crap," he said. "I'm not a good person. You're a saint."

Adele shook her head, looking off. "I said some things last night. Things I didn't realize I meant. But I did mean them."

"We all say things sometimes."

"I wanted him to hurt. I wanted him to feel pain."

"Astounding. You're human? I was beginning to wonder."

She looked up at him again, frowning now to meet his returning smile. "It's not funny," she said.

"No, it's not. Well, maybe a little. People feel that, Adele. All the time. I know I do. Like I said, I don't consider myself that good. But I know you. I've seen you. What you feel isn't nearly as important as how you act. You choose well. You've done it again and again. I've seen you do it again and again. You make the right choice, even if you feel something different."

"I don't always."

"Welcome to the club."

Adele wanted to just fall asleep, leaning against John's chest. She didn't want to move. The warmth of the sunlight felt wonderful against her cheeks. But just then, her phone began to ring. Adele wanted to ignore it. It was probably just Paige. Maybe Father Paul. She didn't want to talk to anyone about the case. Not until she got some sleep. She could only imagine how nice it would feel for her head to hit a pillow.

"You gonna answer that?" John said.

"It's my secret boyfriend," Adele murmured. "I don't want you to know about him."

John snorted. "All right—I'll keep your secret."

Adele chuckled. The phone stopped ringing. But then, nearly instantly, it began to ring again. She frowned, loath to lift her head, but reluctantly, pushing away from John, she pulled her phone from her pocket. Adele glanced at the screen, not recognizing the number. She hesitated and then lifted the device. She could feel John watching her, studying her expression.

"Hello?" Adele said. "Who is this?"

"Agent Sharp?" said a voice. A deep, gruff voice.

"Who is this?"

"Sergeant Rey. Police." He spoke unmistakably in French.

"Where?"

"Paris."

She looked at John.

"Who is it?" John whispered.

"Police," she replied.

"Well, Sergeant, what can I help you with?"

"Is this Agent Adele Sharp?"

"How did you get my number?"

"Your office. Look, I'm afraid I have some news."

Adele felt her heart skip a beat. She was too tired to feel much, but a mounting sense of anxiety twisted in her belly. "Sergeant, you're beginning to worry me. What's the matter?"

"I—apologies, but I think I should tell you in person. How far are you from Paris?"

"I'm in Spain. Is this important? I can be there tomorrow."

He sighed. "*Merde*. Well, maybe we can't wait. I think it might be best if you hear from us. The news is going to pick up on it soon enough."

Now Adele could feel the prickle intensify up her spine. John was watching her, a shrewd look in his hooded eyes. He seemed to realize something was awry. He watched her, quiet now, hands at his side, as if poised for action. But whatever was on the other end of that line, there was nothing he could do about it. And so, facing the inevitability, Adele said, "What is it?"

The gruff voice cleared its throat and then said, "There's no easy way to say this. But your mother's killer just turned himself in."

Adele felt as if her body melted. She wasn't sure when she sat. She wasn't sure when she nearly dropped her phone, fumbled it, and readjusted. All she knew was, a few seconds later, she was sitting on the steps, blinking. John was now at her side, crouched, whispering,

"Are you okay?"

She couldn't really hear him. She understood he was speaking, she could even pick out each word, but they didn't make any sense. "What did you say?" she murmured, her tone completely devoid of anything.

"Your mother's killer turned himself in to the authorities in Paris," said Sergeant Rey. "We need you to come in. He will only speak to you."

The phone fell from her hands. It hit her knee and then hit the steps. Adele felt dizzy again. She swallowed, her throat dry. John was still murmuring in her ear. His hand touched her shoulder. It seemed strange, almost as if she were observing all of this from a different vantage point. As if she wasn't even in her own body.

She cleared her throat and said, as if she were commenting on the breeze, the same way Mr. Segura had spoken, "The strangest thing," she murmured.

"What is it, Adele, you look like you've seen a ghost. What's the matter?"

"The Spade Killer," she said, airily. "How funny. I never thought... Well, so strange."

"Adele, you're scaring me."

She looked at John, studying his face, noticing the bristles on his chin, the five o'clock shadow, the way his eyes flashed. Such a curious specimen. Such a gorgeous man. None of it registered. It was like looking at abstract shapes. She couldn't quite piece them together, noticing his eyes rather than his face. Noticing a tooth instead of teeth. Noticing a hair instead of eyebrows.

Her mind seemed to be short-circuiting.

She could hear someone gasping. It took her second to realize it was her. In, out, rapid. She was shaking now. Shaking so hard, she thought she might bruise her legs against the steps. John came in, hugging her from behind as if trying to shield her from a grenade blast. He held her tight, his body blocking the rest of the world.

"Adele, please," he murmured in her ear, his breath hot. "You're scaring me. I'm scared. What happened? Are you okay? *Who* was that?"

She hesitated, trying to think. None of it really made sense, did it? "I think," she said, in that same emotionless tone, "I think I have to go to Paris. Right now. Right now, John. *Right* now."

156

CHAPTER THIRTY

Adele didn't wait for the cab from the airport to pull to a full stop outside the precinct in the heart of Paris. Even as the tires squealed against the curb, she had already flung open her door and broken into an all-out sprint up the steps to the police station.

John called after her, but she ignored him, gasping, heart pounding, a cold sweat having beaded across her brow.

They hadn't stopped moving since that phone call.

And she wasn't about to slow now.

Adele burst through the front of the police station, which was milling with officers. More than the usual share of law enforcement gathered in corners or by the sergeant's desk, all seemingly in conversation. It felt like a beehive with a buzz of activity all around.

"Where is he?" Adele demanded, her throat tight, her voice hoarse in her own ears. She marched straight up to the sergeant's desk, shouldering roughly past a couple of larger officers who were muttering to each other in low voices.

She caught a couple of words. "Yes... yes, that case."

"...you're sure..."

"...I saw him."

"Why is the Spade Killer turning himself in?"

"I don't know..."

Adele growled, slamming a hand roughly on the plexiglass and pointing a finger at the balding sergeant sitting behind the desk. "Where is he?" she said, louder.

The sergeant looked up, blinking owlishly at her. He seemed to struggle to place her question so she repeated it again, her chest rising and falling rapidly, her shoulders set, her teeth clenched, biting off the word.

At last, the man coughed. "Excuse me," the Parisian said, "but who are you?"

"Adele Sharp. Agent Sharp," she snapped. "I was called by this department. Where is the Spade Killer? Where is he!"

Now a few of the officers gathered near her went quiet, pretending like they weren't eavesdropping but clearly shooting glances in her direction. The man behind the counter folded his hands neatly. "I can ring the captain if you like. He's away right now—sorting things out with your office, in fact. Sergeant Rey is handling the case too, but he's currently on a call upstairs."

"I don't give a shit where he is. I'm here now. I'm not waiting for your captain," she yelled, spittle flecking the counter. She could feel herself coming untethered. She didn't want to sit around jawing with some lickspittle lackey. She needed to see the runty bastard. Needed to see him now.

On the breakneck drive and plane ride over, Adele had been given time to think. Her skin was still crawling and she felt on the verge of screaming and fainting every few seconds. But still, at least a part of her managed to cling to rationality.

Why had the Spade Killer turned himself in? Why now?

What game was he playing at? The news had called him the Spade Killer for murdering people in gardens and parks throughout Paris. Once, the weapon had been thought to be a gardener's spade. The man himself thought of himself as an artist, though. A painter. He'd left horrible patterns carved into the flesh of his victims.

The way he'd cut Elise Romei, Adele's mother. The way he'd brutalized Robert Henry in his own home.

The little bastard had turned himself in. But why?

Something didn't add up.

She didn't have the patience for slow-moving Parisian police in that moment.

"Tell me where he is. Now!" she demanded.

The sergeant behind the desk hesitated, his expression flicking into a frown now. "I really must insist you wait until—"

She howled in frustration, slamming her hand against the counter and wheeling about, stalking down a hallway, past the gathered officers, moving behind the desk.

"Hang on," the sergeant called. "You can't go back there! Wait—wait!"

"Is it here? Down here?" Adele demanded. "Hmm? Do you have him in interrogation?"

"Wait—wait!" the sergeant yelled, desperately.

A police officer moved to intercept her, hand extended, but Adele shoved him hard, hand planting into his chest and sending the man reeling into the wall. "Get off me," she snarled. "Interpol. Get back! Back!"

A couple of other officers moved hesitantly to intervene. She flashed her Interpol credentials, though, followed by her gun, which she left holstered. "Get the hell out of my way," she screamed into the face of a large man blocking her path. "I will cut right through you! Get out!"

She knew she was acting erratically. Knew she was allowing her emotions to get the better of her. But for now, it proved effective. She would have to deal with hurt feelings later. Maybe send a box of chocolates. For now, she shoved past the police officer who, at a command from his sergeant, backed away.

"Please, Agent Sharp! We need the captain back before you go back there!"

She didn't reply. Didn't even look back. She was sick of red tape. Sick of all the ways the Spade Killer had managed to play the lot of them. He'd always had the upper hand. But now here he was, wandering into her home turf.

Something about it was unsettling.

She'd always thought she'd need to catch him.

But he'd taken even that satisfaction away by turning himself in.

Why, though? *Why?*

She approached a row of four interrogation rooms at the end of the hall. Two doors were open. Two closed. But three officers stood outside the second door.

Like signposts pointing toward her destination. Three guards *outside* the room. Hardly usual fare in a precinct. Even in a police headquarters, the little killer had his captors spooked.

She marched straight forward, flashing her credentials again. "Agent Adele Sharp—Interpol and DGSI," she snapped. "Move."

The three officers hesitated. But she didn't wait. She simply reached past them, twisted the lock on the handle, and then shoved open the door before slipping into the gray, bleak room beyond.

The low murmur of officers behind her went mostly unnoticed as the door swung slowly shut behind her on smooth hinges.

The door closed, sending a sudden puff of air through the room, ruffling her hair and cooling her sweaty neck. She stood stock-still for a moment in front of the closed door, her eyes fixed on the small, almost childish figure hunched in one of the plastic chairs.

He was watching her also, one dull eye not quite reflecting the light above. The other twinkling.

He wasn't even handcuffed, his fingers splayed in front of him on the table. He moved his hands cautiously, carefully, treating his fingers as items of great value, the way he glanced at them or twirled them against the table.

Now, as she faced him, cold and motionless, his hands stopped moving. He left them on the table, resting there.

"Hello, Adele," the man said, quietly.

She recognized him. Of course she did. He had more hair than the last time they'd spoken. But it was unmistakable. His features were cold, pallid, his eyes mismatched. He was small, frail even. His fingers were twiggy, brittle almost. Even as he shifted in the chair to face her, he moved with lithe motions, like some stray cat slipping through a chain fence.

He stared at her now, watching her, his eyes darting up and down. For a moment, she thought he was ogling her like some pervert.

She'd experienced this sort of attention before from the more lascivious members of society.

But after a moment, she realized his eyes weren't settling on the usual suspects. Rather, his gaze darted to her ear, flashing as if cataloging. They moved to her hands, then her hair, then down her legs and up again.

At last, he leaned back, sighing as if satisfaction.

"*Magnifique,*" he murmured.

She opened her mouth to reply, but found she didn't want to. Perhaps couldn't. What was there to say to this monster? This man who had murdered her mother. Who had murdered Robert. This man who had tormented her, hunted her. This monster.

He'd turned himself in...

She waited, still watching, but he just watched her back, clearly enjoying the sight judging by the small smile now curving the corners of his lips.

"Stop grinning," she growled. Her voice sounded weak in her own ears. Why hadn't they even cuffed the bastard?

He was here to turn himself in for her mother's murder. Wasn't that what the officer had told her over the phone?

So why was he just sitting there, all pleased with himself?

His smile flashed now, wider. Some of his teeth looked oddly bright as if they'd been replaced or treated with one too many whitening strips.

"Why are you here?" she demanded at last. Even talking to him made her skin crawl. The last time they'd interacted had been beneath a bridge. She'd made promises then. Promises to herself.

He'd managed to escape then. But there were no rivers to jump into now. No escape plans.

Or were there?

160

Instead of answering her question, the painter just watched her, tilting his head ever so slightly, a curious, almost boyish expression on his face.

"Why are you here?" she said, louder now, snarling.

Someone began to pull the interrogation room door open behind her, but she shot her hand out, snatched the handle, and slammed it shut. The person on the other side didn't try again.

The painter continued waiting, folding his hands now, still smiling. So much could be seen in a smile. He clearly knew this. He knew he was taunting her. He was enjoying it.

How many times had he considered this moment?

He'd been sick for a long time, pursuing her for years now.

He'd taken a shot at her father, at John. He'd hunted everything she'd loved out of his sick desire to dismantle her life one piece at a time. One brick torn down, then another, and another.

Now they were face to face, he seemed to be enjoying himself.

Adele took a step forward, toward the interrogation room table. "Why did you turn yourself in. Say something! Say it!"

He just watched her. Though they were in an interrogation room, though they were trapped together, Adele couldn't shake the sensation they were doing this on *his* terms.

As she frowned at him, she noticed his fingers. All of them, spread wide. The ten digits jutting each way. The motion seemed intentional somehow. Ten? Ten what?

She blinked…

And then it hit her like a truck.

Ten years.

More than ten years since he'd murdered her mother.

The statute of limitations in France was up…

She'd always known the only way to prosecute the monster would have been to indict him for more recent murders.

"You think you're clever," she murmured, glaring at his splayed fingers. "You killed Robert, too. That's within the limitations. I'm going to send you to hell, understand me? You're going away forever."

The killer just smirked now, his smile turning to a grin. "Proof?" he murmured.

She blinked, staring at him.

She'd known Robert had been killed by this little monster. He'd teased her about it in the past. But… there hadn't been any physical evidence at the crime scene. He was always careful. He never left anything behind.

"So that's it?" she said, snarling. "You think you're clever? Think you can play? You think you'll turn yourself in for my mother's murder and we won't prosecute, because ten years is up? Is that it? Is this some sort of game to you? You think we don't have evidence you were involved in Robert's death? Hmm? We do! We have evidence!"

He just looked at her for a moment. Then shook his head. "I know your tells, Adele. I know you. You have nothing. Because I didn't do it. Some copycat must have."

Adele just stared at him, gaping.

"I know the error of my ways," he said, nodding but still grinning. "Ten years ago, I reformed. I've never harmed again."

"You attacked my father!" she yelled. "He can identify you."

"Oh? You mean in Germany?" he said, his voice lilting. "This is France, Adele. We don't extradite." He placed a hand over his heart. "*Viva la France.*"

As he spoke, it was beginning to make sense. The little runt had always been bold. She couldn't fault him for that. He'd once bought the apartment across from hers just to watch her, right under her nose.

The statute of limitations was up on her mother's murder. There wasn't physical evidence tying him to Robert's murder. And the attack in Germany wouldn't concern French authorities. They didn't extradite French citizens.

The man continued watching her, beaming now as if reading her thoughts.

"You think you've won, hmm?" Adele said, breathing heavily. "You think you've beaten me?"

He didn't say anything, still smiling, clearly enjoying himself.

"You're making a mistake. Let me tell you—right now. You are making a mistake. You think you know me? You think you know what I'll do?"

He nodded once, but continued his silence.

She snarled. "You were much more talkative the last time we met. What happened? Cat got your tongue? Are you scared, little man? You look scared to me."

She wasn't even sure why she was goading him. It wasn't a tactic. She was simply furious. She'd never felt so much rage in her life. Now she understood what it might be like to be a murderer. In that moment, she didn't care what happened to her, just so long as he suffered.

But even then, amidst the rage, the shock, the fury, the dawning realization of it all, she knew she was missing something.

Why was he just watching her, smirking... as if he were waiting for

162

something? Waiting for what, though?

And then her phone began to ring.

Now the little man looked practically euphoric, leaning in now, grinning so widely she thought his face might split. "I think that's for you," he murmured, pointing toward her pocket. "I will wait. No worries."

Adele kept her expression cold, emotionless. For a moment, out of spite, she considered letting the phone go to voicemail. But the ringing sound seemed to have prompted something in the small man. Almost as if he'd been waiting for this very thing.

So, still glaring daggers at the killer, she reached her hand into her pocket and, realizing her fingers were trembling so badly she almost dropped the device, she lifted it with help from her other hand.

The killer stared pointedly at her shaking fingers—he wanted her to know he saw her fear. He wanted her to feel exposed, vulnerable. Now he did ogle her chest. He licked his lips and winked. She felt exposed, even in a precinct, with backup outside the door. She felt a shiver along her spine. Felt a sense of helplessness she had when she'd first heard about her mother.

She turned, facing the door for a moment, answering the phone.

"What?" she said, her voice shaky as well.

"Adele," said a voice on the other end. It took her a moment to place the voice.

"Lee?" she replied, breathily. Supervising Agent Lee Grant had been the first person to approve the Interpol assignment as a liaison between the agencies. The FBI head was a bit older than Adele, but was also a friend.

"Adele, hey—I'm calling as a courtesy. We got a case over here. The victim's name pinged as a contact of yours."

Adele swallowed. She could feel the small man's eyes fixed on her from behind. Could feel her heart hammering wildly. Could feel the hesitation in the voice on the other line.

A victim? Why was the FBI calling her? Grant was based in California...

Adele turned slowly, frowning at where the painter was sitting, hands crossed now, smiling still. A small, pink tongue probed out, licking his bottom lip faintly before retreating back into his mouth.

"I'm sorry," she said, distractedly. "What?"

"Do you know an Angus McClure?" said Agent Lee quietly. "He's currently living in your old apartment."

"I—I gave the apartment to him," said Adele. "Wait—hang on..." A prickle spread across her skin, starting along her hands and moving up toward her throat. Her ears were buzzing and for a moment, she couldn't hear very well.

"I'm afraid it's bad news, Adele. I'm really, really sorry, honey. Angus was found murdered this morning. It's a mess. I won't go into details, but I can send the report over if you'd like. Do you have any idea who might have done this? We're pulling a blank on the scene."

Adele didn't reply. She just lowered the phone, clicking it off. The call didn't matter now. Angus... Angus was dead. She felt a sob coming to her lips, but spit instead. Hell would freeze over before she let this monster watch her cry. But still, her emotions were a mess, her insides whirring. She could only imagine the horrors that had been done to her old boyfriend. She'd thought they were going to get married. She'd once envisioned a life with him.

Now he was dead too.

Like the rest.

She stared at the small man who was still watching her, like a child examining a worm before raising a magnifying lens to the sun.

He'd done it.

Of course he had.

He'd flown to the US, killed her ex-fiancé, returned, and had turned himself in just so he could watch her. So he could see her reaction.

Worse... he was still smiling, one dull eye unseeing, the other seeing everything.

In his gaze, besides the delight of a pure sadist, besides the enjoyment of the moment, she also saw a cold certainty.

He knew he would get off scot-free for killing her mother and Robert and Angus. All of them were innocent. None of them deserved any of that.

Three victims tied to her. Three more dead.

They had suffered. But the one guilty for it, sitting across from her—he wouldn't suffer a thing. The French wouldn't extradite to Germany *or* America. They'd proven it in the past. The statute had run out on her mother. Robert's case had no evidence.

He'd planned it all. He'd known it all along. And now, sitting across from her, he watched the horrified realization play across her face, still grinning that infuriating little smirk of his.

He'd killed everyone else, but left her alive. She hadn't protected them, hadn't saved them. She was guilty, too, but he let her live. Perhaps that was why. In a way, their blood was also on her hands. Her incompetence. Her inability to catch the monster.

164

She let out a soft breath and slowly approached the table, sliding into the chair across from him, placing her own hands on the table and staring over her knuckles at where the monster sat.

She'd suspected all along it might come down to this.

She'd known it.

He would escape. He'd keep tormenting her until either she was dead...

Or he was.

The path forward seemed clear now.

She swallowed once, facing the man who'd ripped her life to shreds and, in a ghost of a voice, barely above a whisper, not even making eye contact, she stared at the table and said, "This isn't going to end how you think. I get it now. I understand. You want to play the game your way?"

She looked up, feeling liquid rage bruiting through her bloodstream. "All right," she murmured. "We'll play it your way."

NOW AVAILABLE!

LEFT TO LURE
(An Adele Sharp Mystery—Book 12)

"When you think that life cannot get better, Blake Pierce comes up with another masterpiece of thriller and mystery! This book is full of twists and the end brings a surprising revelation. I strongly recommend this book to the permanent library of any reader that enjoys a very well written thriller."
--Books and Movie Reviews, Roberto Mattos (re Almost Gone)

LEFT TO LURE is book #12 in a new FBI thriller series featuring Adele Sharp (the series begins with LEFT TO DIE, book #1) by USA Today bestselling author Blake Pierce, whose #1 bestseller Once Gone (a free download) has received over 1,000 five star reviews.

A body is found strung up at the Leaning Tower of Pisa, leaving the local police baffled, and assuming it's an isolated incident. Until tragedy strikes again, at an equally unusual setting.

FBI Agent Adele Sharp, haunted by the resurfacing of her mother's killer, is called into investigate this unsual serial killer, as he crosses borders into other countries and evades all the police. But what is the connection between all the victims? Is this killer more psychotic than she thought? And can she piece together the clues, enter his mind, and unravel the mystery before more innocent lives are lost?

An action-packed mystery series of international intrigue and riveting suspense, LEFT TO LURE will leave you turning pages late into the night.

Book #13 in the series—LEFT TO CRAVE—is now also available!

Blake Pierce

Blake Pierce is the USA Today bestselling author of the RILEY PAGE mystery series, which includes seventeen books. Blake Pierce is also the author of the MACKENZIE WHITE mystery series, comprising fourteen books; of the AVERY BLACK mystery series, comprising six books; of the KERI LOCKE mystery series, comprising five books; of the MAKING OF RILEY PAIGE mystery series, comprising six books; of the KATE WISE mystery series, comprising seven books; of the CHLOE FINE psychological suspense mystery, comprising six books; of the JESSE HUNT psychological suspense thriller series, comprising nineteen books; of the AU PAIR psychological suspense thriller series, comprising three books; of the ZOE PRIME mystery series, comprising six books; of the ADELE SHARP mystery series, comprising thirteen books, of the EUROPEAN VOYAGE cozy mystery series, comprising four books; of the new LAURA FROST FBI suspense thriller, comprising six books (and counting); of the new ELLA DARK FBI suspense thriller, comprising nine books (and counting); of the A YEAR IN EUROPE cozy mystery series, comprising nine books, of the AVA GOLD mystery series, comprising six books (and counting); and of the RACHEL GIFT mystery series, comprising six books (and counting).

An avid reader and lifelong fan of the mystery and thriller genres, Blake loves to hear from you, so please feel free to visit www.blakepierceauthor.com to learn more and stay in touch.

BOOKS BY BLAKE PIERCE

RACHEL GIFT MYSTERY SERIES
HER LAST WISH (Book #1)
HER LAST CHANCE (Book #2)
HER LAST HOPE (Book #3)
HER LAST FEAR (Book #4)
HER LAST CHOICE (Book #5)
HER LAST BREATH (Book #6)

AVA GOLD MYSTERY SERIES
CITY OF PREY (Book #1)
CITY OF FEAR (Book #2)
CITY OF BONES (Book #3)
CITY OF GHOSTS (Book #4)
CITY OF DEATH (Book #5)
CITY OF VICE (Book #6)

A YEAR IN EUROPE
A MURDER IN PARIS (Book #1)
DEATH IN FLORENCE (Book #2)
VENGEANCE IN VIENNA (Book #3)
A FATALITY IN SPAIN (Book #4)

ELLA DARK FBI SUSPENSE THRILLER
GIRL, ALONE (Book #1)
GIRL, TAKEN (Book #2)
GIRL, HUNTED (Book #3)
GIRL, SILENCED (Book #4)
GIRL, VANISHED (Book 5)
GIRL ERASED (Book #6)
GIRL, FORSAKEN (Book #7)
GIRL, TRAPPED (Book #8)
GIRL, EXPENDABLE (Book #9)

LAURA FROST FBI SUSPENSE THRILLER
ALREADY GONE (Book #1)

ALREADY SEEN (Book #2)
ALREADY TRAPPED (Book #3)
ALREADY MISSING (Book #4)
ALREADY DEAD (Book #5)
ALREADY TAKEN (Book #6)

EUROPEAN VOYAGE COZY MYSTERY SERIES
MURDER (AND BAKLAVA) (Book #1)
DEATH (AND APPLE STRUDEL) (Book #2)
CRIME (AND LAGER) (Book #3)
MISFORTUNE (AND GOUDA) (Book #4)
CALAMITY (AND A DANISH) (Book #5)
MAYHEM (AND HERRING) (Book #6)

ADELE SHARP MYSTERY SERIES
LEFT TO DIE (Book #1)
LEFT TO RUN (Book #2)
LEFT TO HIDE (Book #3)
LEFT TO KILL (Book #4)
LEFT TO MURDER (Book #5)
LEFT TO ENVY (Book #6)
LEFT TO LAPSE (Book #7)
LEFT TO VANISH (Book #8)
LEFT TO HUNT (Book #9)
LEFT TO FEAR (Book #10)
LEFT TO PREY (Book #11)
LEFT TO LURE (Book #12)
LEFT TO CRAVE (Book #13)

THE AU PAIR SERIES
ALMOST GONE (Book#1)
ALMOST LOST (Book #2)
ALMOST DEAD (Book #3)

ZOE PRIME MYSTERY SERIES
FACE OF DEATH (Book#1)
FACE OF MURDER (Book #2)
FACE OF FEAR (Book #3)
FACE OF MADNESS (Book #4)
FACE OF FURY (Book #5)

FACE OF DARKNESS (Book #6)

A JESSIE HUNT PSYCHOLOGICAL SUSPENSE SERIES
THE PERFECT WIFE (Book #1)
THE PERFECT BLOCK (Book #2)
THE PERFECT HOUSE (Book #3)
THE PERFECT SMILE (Book #4)
THE PERFECT LIE (Book #5)
THE PERFECT LOOK (Book #6)
THE PERFECT AFFAIR (Book #7)
THE PERFECT ALIBI (Book #8)
THE PERFECT NEIGHBOR (Book #9)
THE PERFECT DISGUISE (Book #10)
THE PERFECT SECRET (Book #11)
THE PERFECT FAÇADE (Book #12)
THE PERFECT IMPRESSION (Book #13)
THE PERFECT DECEIT (Book #14)
THE PERFECT MISTRESS (Book #15)
THE PERFECT IMAGE (Book #16)
THE PERFECT VEIL (Book #17)
THE PERFECT INDISCRETION (Book #18)
THE PERFECT RUMOR (Book #19)

CHLOE FINE PSYCHOLOGICAL SUSPENSE SERIES
NEXT DOOR (Book #1)
A NEIGHBOR'S LIE (Book #2)
CUL DE SAC (Book #3)
SILENT NEIGHBOR (Book #4)
HOMECOMING (Book #5)
TINTED WINDOWS (Book #6)

KATE WISE MYSTERY SERIES
IF SHE KNEW (Book #1)
IF SHE SAW (Book #2)
IF SHE RAN (Book #3)
IF SHE HID (Book #4)
IF SHE FLED (Book #5)
IF SHE FEARED (Book #6)
IF SHE HEARD (Book #7)

BEFORE HE STALKS (Book #13)
BEFORE HE HARMS (Book #14)

AVERY BLACK MYSTERY SERIES
CAUSE TO KILL (Book #1)
CAUSE TO RUN (Book #2)
CAUSE TO HIDE (Book #3)
CAUSE TO FEAR (Book #4)
CAUSE TO SAVE (Book #5)
CAUSE TO DREAD (Book #6)

KERI LOCKE MYSTERY SERIES
A TRACE OF DEATH (Book #1)
A TRACE OF MURDER (Book #2)
A TRACE OF VICE (Book #3)
A TRACE OF CRIME (Book #4)
A TRACE OF HOPE (Book #5)

Made in United States
Orlando, FL
04 January 2023

28106309R00098